P9-BYW-872

"I was damn proud of you today, Nan."

"That's the nicest thing you've ever said to me."

Her words made David's chest ache. "I have lots of other things to tell you. Whenever you're ready to hear them." He peered into her lovely face, drew in her fresh scent and fought to remember why he shouldn't take her in his arms and crush her close.

"David?" she whispered, laying her hand on his chest. A warning? An invitation? His heart pounded in his ears. "The kids are waiting in the car."

Her words sliced through the haze of his mind. He closed his eyes for a moment but still clutched her hand, unwilling to break the connection, waiting for sense to overtake his desire.

He should be grateful the kids were waiting. If they weren't, he'd have given in to his need to kiss her. And from the look in her eyes, she wouldn't have stopped him.

Dear Reader,

Well, the wait is over—*New York Times* bestselling author Diana Palmer is back, and Special Edition has got her! In *Carrera's Bride*, another in Ms. Palmer's enormously popular LONG, TALL TEXANS miniseries, an innocent Jacobsville girl on a tropical getaway finds herself in need of protection—and gets it from an infamous casino owner who is not all that he appears! I think you'll find this one was well worth the wait....

We're drawing near the end of our in-series continuity THE PARKS EMPIRE. This month's entry is *The Marriage Act* by Elissa Ambrose, in which a shy secretary learns that her one night of sleeping with the enemy has led to unexpected consequences. Next up is *The Sheik & the Princess Bride* by Susan Mallery, in which a woman hired to teach a prince how to fly finds herself *his* student, as well, as he gives her lessons...in love! In *A Baby on the Ranch*, part of Stella Bagwell's popular MEN OF THE WEST miniseries, a single mother-to-be finds her long-lost family—and, just possibly, the love of her life. And a single man in the market for household help finds himself about to take on the role of husband—and father of four—in Penny Richards's *Wanted: One Father*. Oh, and speaking of single parents—a lonely widow with a troubled adolescent son finds the solution to both her problems in her late husband's law-enforcement partner, in *The Way to a Woman's Heart* by Carol Voss.

So enjoy, and come back next month for six wonderful selections from Silhouette Special Edition.

Happy Thanksgiving!

Gail Chasan
Senior Editor

Please address questions and book requests to:
Silhouette Reader Service
U.S.: 3010 Walden Ave., P.O. Box 1325, Buffalo, NY 14269
Canadian: P.O. Box 609, Fort Erie, Ont. L2A 5X3

The Way to a Woman's Heart

CAROL VOSS

SPECIAL EDITION

Published by Silhouette Books

America's Publisher of Contemporary Romance

If you purchased this book without a cover you should be aware that this book is stolen property. It was reported as "unsold and destroyed" to the publisher, and neither the author nor the publisher has received any payment for this "stripped book."

To Ann, whose faith never wavered; to Gil, who supported before he believed; to Kathy, who inspired; to Jude, who encouraged; to Pam Hopkins, who led the way; to Patience Smith, who made it happen, and to Susan Litman and Gail Chason, who pulled it off. Thank you from the bottom of my heart.

 SILHOUETTE BOOKS

ISBN 0-373-24650-1

THE WAY TO A WOMAN'S HEART

Copyright © 2004 by Carol Voss

All rights reserved. Except for use in any review, the reproduction or utilization of this work in whole or in part in any form by any electronic, mechanical or other means, now known or hereafter invented, including xerography, photocopying and recording, or in any information storage or retrieval system, is forbidden without the written permission of the editorial office, Silhouette Books, 233 Broadway, New York, NY 10279 U.S.A.

All characters in this book have no existence outside the imagination of the author and have no relation whatsoever to anyone bearing the same name or names. They are not even distantly inspired by any individual known or unknown to the author, and all incidents are pure invention.

This edition published by arrangement with Harlequin Books S.A.

® and TM are trademarks of Harlequin Books S.A., used under license. Trademarks indicated with ® are registered in the United States Patent and Trademark Office, the Canadian Trade Marks Office and in other countries.

Visit Silhouette Books at www.eHarlequin.com

Printed in U.S.A.

CAROL VOSS

In the years between graduating from business college and achieving a liberal arts degree from the University of Wisconsin-Green Bay, Carol Voss worked in a variety of businesses, married, raised three children and collected a few rejection letters from magazines when the voices in her head insisted on being heard. When she began writing romance, the voices began to sing. She couldn't be happier that *The Way to a Woman's Heart* found a home with Silhouette Special Edition. Carol lives near Madison, Wisconsin, with her creative husband, her two vibrant Border collies and her two supervisory cats. Besides writing, she loves reading, walking, yoga, flower gardening, traveling and most of all, her home and family. She would love to hear from readers at her Web site at www.specialauthors.com.

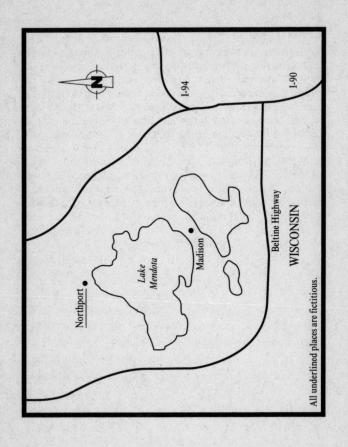

WISCONSIN

I-94

I-90

Beltine Highway

Lake
Mendota

Madison

Northport

All underlined places are fictitious.

Chapter One

Ignoring the knot of tension in his stomach, Dane County sheriff's deputy David Elliott cruised slowly down Maple Street past Nan Kramer's green-shuttered ranch house. Usually, she had a light on when he drove by at midnight. But not tonight. He scanned the house and yard for any sign of trouble as he always did.

He thought about the family sleeping safely inside the house. He thought about Nan. About her soft laugh, the incredible zest for life she'd once had. His heart ached for her and her three fatherless kids.

It should never have happened.

The pain in his fingers reminded him to ease his grip on the steering wheel as he quashed the memory that always hovered close enough to swamp him. Remembering that fateful night didn't do anybody any good. Not his dead partner, not Nan and the kids. And most of all, not himself.

Breathing in the pungent, late-August scent of algae from nearby Lake Mendota, he turned the corner and drove his Jeep Wrangler onto tiny Northport, Wisconsin's Main Street toward home and a cold bottle of beer. He flexed his tight shoulder muscles, very aware that six twelve-hour shifts in six days were getting to him.

A sinister flurry of movement in the alley behind Harper's Drugstore caught his eye. Adrenaline shot through his body like a bullet. Damn. Getting home would have to wait.

He slammed on the brakes and threw the Jeep into reverse. Tires squealing, the vehicle jetted backward. A hard twist on the steering wheel swerved the Jeep's rear end into the middle of the street, its headlights beaming down the alley.

The glare caught a three-kid pyramid poised atop a makeshift perch under a second-story window. David jammed the gear shift into neutral and pulled the parking brake, then shoved open the door and leaped from the vehicle.

"It's a cop!" The bottom layer of the pyramid collapsed. Two figures jumped, boards from their perch clattering noisily to the ground. The two kids raced for the shadows of a nearby house.

"Hey! I can't get down!" The pyramid's top section hung from the high window by his arms, twisting his scrawny body to see what had happened. He was dangling too high above the ground to jump without risking at least a sprained ankle.

Clanking garbage cans rattled from the darkness. Hoping the kid had strong enough arms to hang on, David charged toward the commotion.

In the dim streetlight, the two runners darted across the neighboring yard and split off in opposite directions. He sprinted after the kid in the white T-shirt, the easier target in the dark.

David slowed his pace at the corner streetlight. An abandoned barn-like building, its windows and doors boarded up, towered on one side of the street. The kid could be hiding in there. But the bevy of parked cars at the gas station across the corner looked like a better place.

He listened for any giveaway sound. Nothing but the rustling of leaves, the buzz of insects circling the streetlight and his own rapid breathing. Damn. Better go see if the third kid was still hanging from the window.

He turned and jogged back to the scene of the crime. The kid still dangled there, flailing his legs this way and that like a snagged helicopter. He wore tennis shoes, denim cutoffs and a scarlet T-shirt and looked about ten years old. Way too young for burglary. Like there was any good age? David stopped under the young hoodlum.

''Get me down.'' The little thief's voice warbled as if he was on the verge of tears.

Stepping closer, David's shoes crunched splintered glass from the broken window above. He gripped the boy's skinny legs and guided his feet. "You can let go. I've got you." The kid's weight, not more than seventy-five pounds, sank onto David's shoulders. He swung the boy to the ground and jerked him around.

The kid stared up at him with somber gray eyes.

Corry's eyes.

David sucked in a breath of dread. "Justin?"

The soft, golden curls he remembered had been shorn short, the playful smile replaced by a scowl— but the boy was Justin Kramer, all right. The knot in David's stomach twisted painfully. When had the kid taken up breaking and entering?

Justin squeezed his eyes shut, then opened them wide as if he didn't trust his vision. "David? Why are *you* here?"

"Just luck, I guess." He'd give anything *not* to be here. If only he hadn't noticed the commotion in the alley, if he hadn't been compelled to check it out, he could be home right now enjoying a cold bottle of beer. Instead, he stood looking into the guilty gray eyes of his dead partner's son.

And worse, he would have to tell Nan.

Justin's shoulders slumped. Hanging his head, he concentrated on David's shoes. "So I'm stupid."

The boy looked pathetic. His face was dirt streaked, his eyes suspiciously damp. But pity wouldn't do the kid any good. Besides, David was angry, damned angry. He released him. "Stupid doesn't even come close."

"It's not what it looks like."

"Don't even bother to make up a lie. I've heard them all."

Justin rolled his eyes to look up at David. "We weren't gonna steal any drugs or anything. We were hungry. We wanted some chips and stuff."

David groaned. "You expect me to believe a story like that? If you wanted food, why'd you pick Harper's instead of, say, Ben's gas station?"

"We thought we could climb in through the alley window and nobody would see us."

The innocence in the boy's wide eyes didn't fool him for a minute. "We?"

"Me and a couple guys." Justin scuffed his shoe in the gravel.

"Do these guys have names?"

"Do you have to tell my mom?"

Regret chilled David despite the hot night. He'd rather face a firing squad than lay more heartache on Nan's doorstep. "If there was any other way, I sure wouldn't." He paused, looking at Justin. "Your friends' names. What are they?"

Justin's chin quivered a little, but he squared his shoulders and looked David straight in the eye. "I can't tell you that."

Wonderful. Squelching the urge to shake some sense into the kid, David jammed his hands into his pockets. "I'm sorry you feel that way. Does that mean you're planning to take all the blame for this little caper? It might get kind of lonely."

"You're not going to arrest me, are you?"

Good question. What *was* he going to do with him? "Breaking and entering is against the law."

"Mom thinks I'm asleep. She's gonna be really mad." Justin focused on the gravel again.

Oh, hell. For once, Nan had turned in before midnight. He would have to wake her up and tell her Justin sneaked out after she'd tucked him safely in bed. She'd been hurt enough.

His mind filled with the vision of her at Corry's funeral two years ago, huddled with grief and peering at him through pain-stunned eyes. The vision that haunted him night and day.

He wanted to throttle the kid. "Why'd you do some idiot thing like this? You know better. Do you have any idea how much this is going to hurt your mom? Do you?"

"I didn't think—"

"You got that right. Come on, get in the Jeep. I'll take you home." The knot in his gut wrenched without mercy. He'd done his best to protect Nan, from a distance, ever since Corry died, but he couldn't protect her from this. For two long years, he'd dreaded facing her. He couldn't have imagined these circumstances.

Jamming his fists deeper into his pockets, he strode resolutely to his Jeep, a sullen Justin jogging to keep up.

Bells jangled insistently through Nan Kramer's exhausted mind. She fought through sleep to foggy consciousness. Prying Brenda's little arm from its stranglehold around her neck, she squinted at the illuminated numbers of the clock radio on the bedside table. Twelve-thirty. She'd been asleep only half an hour.

Had the doorbell really awakened her, or was it her nightmare again? The nightmare always began with the doorbell.

Trembling with a sudden chill, she clambered up and reached for her white, terry robe draped across the foot of the bed. She had to check on the kids. She needed to make sure they were safe.

"Mommy," Brenda wailed shrilly from the bed.

"Everything's all right, sweetie. I'm going to check on Melody and Justin."

Again, bells clanged through the still house, jolting her nerves like a gun blast. It *was* the doorbell. Who could be at her door at this hour? Fear pierced her mind, carrying her to the night Corry died. The night the ring of the doorbell changed her life forever.

"Who's here, Mommy?"

Nan drew in a deliberate breath of calm. "I'll find out. You go back to sleep, okay?"

"But it's dark."

"No, it's not. The night-light is on in the hall."

"Don't leave me, Mommy." Brenda's shrill little voice hovered close to tears.

"Let's get you back into your own bed. Then Melody will be with you." Nan grasped the small, warm hand and helped her five-year-old scramble out of the big bed. Together they groped their way toward the dim light in the hall. The doorbell jangled yet again. She could swear it got louder with each assault.

"Mo-om," Melody's sleepy voice demanded from the girls' room. "Who's at the door?"

Reaching the hall, Nan bent and quickly hugged Brenda's warm, Mr.-Bubble-scented body. "I don't know, Melody. Please take Brenda so I can find out."

Thirteen-year-old Melody clutched Brenda. "Do you want me to come with you to answer the door?" Her voice sounded hushed, fearful.

"No. Just take Brenda. I'm sure it's only a neighbor." She was sure of no such thing, but she knew Melody remembered that awful night as vividly as Nan did, and she had to say something to reassure her daughter. She padded down the hall and into the living room, the worn oak floor cool beneath her feet.

A tall, dark shadow loomed outside the curtained window of the front door.

She stopped. Chills crept over her skin. A scream echoed through her mind. The man outside her door would tell her some awful thing had happened, and her life would never be the same. *No. Please. Not again.* Drawing in a shaky breath, she clung to reason.

This wasn't her nightmare. This was real.

"Who is it?" Why wouldn't her voice work? "Who is it?"

"David Elliot," a smooth baritone answered.

David? She'd barely caught a glimpse of him since the funeral two years ago. Why would he suddenly show up now? What was he doing on her front porch in the middle of the night?

"I'm sorry to wake you, Nan, but there's a problem." His voice was forceful, his words clipped. He sounded so official.

She stared at the door. She didn't want to know.

"Nan? Are you still there?" Concern softened the official ring in his voice.

She couldn't just stand there. She had to open the door. She yanked the robe's belt firmly around her middle, switched on the lights and turned the dead bolt. Raking her fingers through her short curls with one hand, she pulled the door open with the other.

And faced her eleven-year-old son.

"Justin!" Nan's heart took a dive into the pit of her stomach. Grasping the door frame for support, she stared unbelieving, trying to understand. She did a quick once-over, checking for any sign of injuries. No blood. He seemed intact. But his eyes looked give-away moist, and dirt streaked his cheeks. "What's going on?"

Justin raised agitated gray eyes to meet hers. "Don't worry, Mom. I'm okay."

"What are you doing out here? You were in bed!"

Shifting from one tennie-clad foot to the other, Justin stared at the porch floor.

David cleared his throat.

Nan looked up at the tall, brown-and-tan-uniformed officer who'd been a good friend to her and Corry what seemed like so very long ago.

Tension emanated from his ramrod-straight physique, and his short dark hair clung damply to his frowning forehead. His brown eyes held a mixture of pain and warmth. "Let's step inside. Justin's in a little trouble, I'm afraid."

She clutched at her robe, clasping it tightly closed at her neck. Moving back, she allowed them to step into the room. "What kind of trouble?"

He drew in a deep breath. "You want to tell your mom about it, Justin?"

Her son shifted his weight and continued to glare at the floor.

She waited for him to explain, barely daring to breathe, but no words came from Justin's lips. What had he done that he couldn't even tell her about? She focused on David for an explanation.

Glowering at Justin, David swallowed and drew in another deep breath. "He and two other boys broke one of Harper's windows. I caught the boys trying to hoist Justin through."

She closed her eyes and attempted to make sense of his words. Justin had seemed to get angrier as time passed after his father's death, no matter how hard she'd tried to help him. Opening her eyes, she stared at her son, nearly sinking under the weight of fear for her child.

"I'm sorry to bring you bad news."

The familiar caring in David's voice almost started the tears that never seemed far away. But this was no time to cry. "Justin, I can't believe this. You actually sneaked out of the house? What were you thinking?"

Justin bit his lip.

David gave her a look over her son's head, a look filled with misery and silent apology. "The other boys ran away, but Justin doesn't seem to remember their names.''

Nan looked at her son. ''You can't protect your friends, Justin. Tell Deputy Elliott who the boys are.''

''I can't snitch, Mom.''

She drew in an exasperated breath of air. ''Loyalty is a good thing, but it has to work both ways. You're in trouble with the police. And your friends are leaving you holding the bag here.''

Justin's chin jutted, a sure sign he'd dug in his heels.

Nan looked into David's troubled eyes. ''Have you arrested him?''

He shook his head. ''Not exactly. But I can't drop it, either. I'll have to write up a report. This is serious, and Justin has to face the consequences.''

He didn't have to tell her the seriousness of the situation. She'd been married to a deputy for twelve years. She knew how unbending the law could be. Obviously, that was a lesson her son needed to learn.

''Who is it, Mom?'' Melody yelled from her room.

''It's okay, Melody. Go to sleep.'' She hoped her daughter didn't pick up on the tremor in her voice and decide to come out to see for herself that everything was all right.

David laid his hand on Justin's shoulder as though he'd made up his mind. ''It's late. Why don't you go to bed, Justin? Your mom and I need to talk about this.''

Justin's gray eyes darted to Nan for confirmation.

She nodded, squelching the ache in her heart those perplexed gray eyes could impose. "I'll be in later."

Head down, Justin bolted past her, the thud of his tennies pounding the worn oak floors all the way to his room.

She could hardly believe Justin sneaked out of bed. That he'd broken into Mr. Harper's store seemed impossible. She wanted to follow him to his room and demand he tell her the names of the boys he'd been with. But anger never got her anywhere with Justin.

A hot rush of nausea flooded her. Pressing her fingers tightly to her lips, she closed her eyes and concentrated on swallowing rapidly. She couldn't be sick. Or faint. David would think she'd lost all control.

He grasped her upper arm. "Are you all right?"

The nausea subsiding enough to allow her to breathe, she opened her eyes and nodded uncertainly. "I should talk with him." Besides being angry with Justin, she was downright afraid for him. How could she protect him when he seemed bent on racing helter-skelter down a path of self-destruction?

"Not tonight. It'll do him good to worry about what he's done."

David worked with teenagers, but what did he know about parenting? He didn't know how much Justin missed his father or how silent her son had become. David hadn't held him, sobbing uncontrollably after one of his nightmares, nor awakened to hear him sniffling quietly in his bed.

She didn't have answers to Justin's questions. All she could do was hold him.

She'd tried hard to be mother and father to her little boy, but she'd made mistakes. Too many mistakes. "I shouldn't have moved the kids out of the city after Corry died. Justin has never adjusted. He's had trouble in school, trouble making new friends. But he's never gotten in this kind of trouble before."

"Don't blame yourself, Nan. It might be worse if you'd stayed in Madison."

It *could* be worse. She knew that, but still she trembled as if she was coming down with the flu. She had to get herself under control, so she could deal with this.

"Don't you dare fold up on me. You need to sit down. You're white as a sheet." He stepped closer, slipping his arm around her for support. His hard, muscular body pressed against her.

His heat made her feel feminine and self-conscious, which only added to her embarrassment at her inability to cope. She tried to laugh, but the strangled whimper sounded more like a sob.

"Come on," he said gruffly, turning her into the room. Lifting her half off her feet, he propelled her across the room to the couch.

Sinking into its soft embrace, she ignored Brenda's backpack and the crayons that spilled across one end.

"Put your head on your knees." No mistaking the ring of a lawman's authority in his deep baritone.

"I'm fine," she protested.

"Put your head down," he commanded, thrusting his hand into her curls and pushing her head down.

His touch jarred her nerves and gave her the oddest

sensation deep inside. Obediently, she bent at the waist and rested her forehead on her knees.

"Stay there while I get you some water."

Tears stung her eyelids. What a mess. Sucking in a gulp of air, she tried not to think about how ridiculous she looked. But she stayed that way until she heard David walk back into the room. Then she straightened, smoothed her hair and pressed her cool palms to her hot cheeks.

He held out a glass of water. "Any better?"

She'd forgotten the velvet warmth in his dark, intense eyes, eyes filled with caring and concern. Her composure returning, she nodded and accepted the glass. "Please sit down, David." She gestured to the scuffed, leather recliner near the couch. Corry's chair.

David lowered his lanky frame into the chair.

Suddenly the room seemed crowded with his presence; with his heat and the male scent of action and fresh sweat. Not too surprising considering that in the nearly two years she and the children had lived here, a man had never sat in her living room. And this man looked as if he'd rather be just about anywhere else.

His long, lean muscles tensed as if poised for flight. Tension and energy radiated from him as if he defied nature to sit still. He'd always been such a physical man, much more at home swimming or water-skiing than sitting anywhere. She should try to put him at ease, but she didn't know how when she was so ill at ease herself. She took a gulp of cool water.

A black blur raced from the kitchen and landed in David's lap. His eyes widened in surprise. Staring down at the black cat, he recovered admirably. "Hello, Sheba."

Nan smiled, glad for the distraction. "Sheba remembers you. She always hides from strangers."

A muscle worked in David's strong jaw, and he didn't meet her eyes. He silently stroked the cat, his long fingers dwarfing the pet. Sheba purred ecstatically, sashaying back and forth, swishing her tail plume in his face.

David looked older, sadder and very uncomfortable. And so was she. Where was the easy camaraderie they'd shared in the past?

So much had changed since Corry died. Friends with whom the Kramers had shared happy times seemed to find it hard to communicate with her now. They wanted to fix things that could never be fixed. Nobody knew what to say. But David had been such a good friend, she'd been surprised at his desertion. And she never expected to feel this awkward with him.

He kept his head bent over the purring cat. "I'm sorry I haven't stopped by. I should have tried to help you and the kids after Corry died."

The pain in his voice clutched Nan's heart, a hush settling where her own pain responded. She couldn't deny she'd felt betrayed when he never came around after the funeral. One minute she'd had a loving husband and a loyal and trusted friend in David. When Corry died, she'd lost them both. She'd been angry. With Corry for dying. With David for deserting her. With life mostly, for treating her with such disdain. Such unfairness.

But life hadn't been kind to David, either. He'd loved Corry, too. Obviously, he hadn't wanted to be around Corry's family. But his absence had hurt. "We've missed you."

He stroked the cat, a muscle in his jaw working. "I couldn't accept what happened."

She nodded, instinctively reaching for his hand and clasping it in her own. "There was nothing you could do."

Grasping her hand, he lifted his eyes to meet her gaze. His eyes still burned with the elusive quality that had always intrigued her, made her wonder what he was thinking. His skin was warm, rough and his touch seemed to transfer some of his energy to her. He cleared his throat. "I should have gone in first that night."

Sadness washed through her, heavy with her own bitter questions after Corry's death. "He was the seasoned deputy. And we both know he always went by the book."

David closed his eyes for a moment. "But I wouldn't have left dependents."

Her heart ached for him. For her children. For herself. "Let it go, David. It's over."

"It will never be over." He shook his head slowly. "Not for you and the kids. And not for me." Squeezing her hand, he stared into space, obviously fighting to control his tumultuous emotions. "Maybe I can help with Justin. I've been working with at-risk teens, trying to show them they have alternatives to drugs and guns. Maybe I can do something for Justin, if you're okay with it.''

Alarm zinged straight to her core. "Drugs and guns? Justin?''

David gazed steadily into her eyes. "Maybe not yet. But the kids who ran away tonight were bigger, probably a couple of years older than Justin. I'll bet peer pressure had a lot to do with his behavior tonight.''

She didn't want to deal with her little boy being in trouble, but she had to face facts. She knew that. Before it was too late. And David had been successful with kids. An occasional article in the newspapers, along with friends' comments, had kept her informed.

"Justin and I used to have fun together. Maybe I can take him out in my boat, like Corry and I used to do.''

Her own memories of Corry had only recently dimmed enough to allow her to remember him without tears. She wasn't sure if reminding Justin of how it used to be when his father was alive would be good for him. "I don't know. Being with you might stir up painful memories.''

He leaned forward, a frown creasing his brow, intensity in his dark eyes. "Maybe it's time to face those memories. They're good ones. They shouldn't be locked away like something sinister.''

Nan drew in a deep breath. "Maybe. But memories bring questions that can't be answered. Like why did everything have to change?''

His warm fingers stroked her hand. "I...''

She shouldn't have been so blunt. She peered at him

apologetically. "I appreciate your offer, David, really I do. But I need time to think about all this."

He gave her an understanding nod and released her hand. "You can call me tomorrow. I have some time off so I'll be home all day." He set Sheba on the floor, took a pad with attached pen from his shirt pocket and jotted some numbers. Standing, he held out the small piece of paper. "If I'm working outside, leave a message and I'll get back to you."

She accepted the paper and followed him to the door, his broad body shutting out the room, his shoulders thrown back in a posture that showed he was ready to face the world head-on. She'd forgotten how powerfully he moved.

He turned to her, his warm brown eyes searching her face. "I'm only trying to help, but if you decide you don't want me to get involved with Justin, I'll understand."

Something was keeping her from accepting David's offer. Was she denying that Justin needed that kind of help? Or was she guarding her emotions by keeping a distance from her old friend? After all, he was a deputy. And he could be killed in the line of duty just like Corry had been. "I'll try to figure out what I think will be best for him."

He laid his hand on her shoulder as if to reassure her. "It's harder for a boy to learn how to be a man when he doesn't have a father to teach him."

His big hand felt so good, so familiar. His touch conveyed the warmth and care she'd missed so much since Corry's death. Always-waiting tears surged for release, but she swallowed hard and forced them back. Not trusting her voice enough to speak, she nodded her agreement.

An ironic little smile softened the taut line of his mouth. "Life has dealt Justin a rotten hand. I can't blame him for acting out." Turning abruptly, he strode through the door.

Nan locked up, pushed off the light switches and walked dismally down the dimly lit hall to Justin's room.

Her heart contracted at the sight of the small, tensely waiting figure lying so still, the sheet drawn up over most of his face, his hand poised on purring Sheba cuddled to his chest.

She wanted to gather her little boy into her arms and rock him and sing to him until he fell asleep. But those days were past. And with them, the small problems that could be cured with a kiss or a hug of encouragement.

She sat down on the bed and caressed his slight shoulder. "Good night, Justin. We'll talk in the morning."

He didn't stir or answer. He lay there. So still. So confused. So alone.

Clasping her hand to her mouth, she stifled a sob. She rushed from the room, stumbled down the hall to her own room and closed the door behind her. Groping for the lamp, she knocked something off the bedside table. Glass crashed at her feet. *Oh, please don't let the girls wake up.* She couldn't deal with them right now.

She found the lamp switch. Vision blurred by tears, she focused on the fragments of the shattered crystal bud vase on the floor. Corry's gift after Brenda's birth. Now shattered like her heart. And just as impossible to mend.

Avoiding the glass slivers, she crumpled into bed and buried her face in her pillow. She hadn't felt so alone since Corry died. Alone and confused and afraid. What was she going to do to reach her son?

Sitting in his Jeep in front of Nan's house, David gripped the steering wheel with a vengeance. A light glowed from behind her filmy curtain. She probably couldn't sleep. Just as he wouldn't be able to.

Since Corry'd died, David had imagined facing Nan a thousand times. He'd decided he wasn't ready; that he would probably never be ready. He'd been right.

He slammed the steering wheel with his fists, grateful for the pain that jolted him. He deserved pain.

Corry had treated him like an equal when David had been a green rookie. He'd taught David how to handle himself so he wouldn't get his head blown off. Then Corry had insisted David back him up at the drug bust that awful night. And Corry had charged in first.

Familiar rage overwhelmed him. Shutting his eyes to block the vision of Corry slumping to the ground, David shoved back, his head hitting the seat with a thud.

He should have taken the bullet that night, not Corry with a wife and family to take care of. Not Corry, who hadn't understood that cops shouldn't have dependents. But David knew; he'd learned that lesson in the countless nights he'd lain awake listening to his mother's muffled sobs after his dad was killed in the line of duty.

Of course, his dad's shooting happened in New York City where police officers were killed more frequently than in Dane County, Wisconsin. Corry had been only the third sheriff's deputy killed on duty in the department's history. But his death had corroborated what David had known all along. Cops had no business having families.

Light still glowed from Nan's window. Reaching for the key in the ignition, David thought of her wrestling with the problem Justin had dumped on her. She'd seemed so weighed down, so afraid, and he'd seen no fire in her eyes. His heart expanded until he couldn't breathe. Maybe he should stay near her. Just until she turned out the light.

He'd stayed nearby ever since Corry's shooting, to protect her and the kids from whatever dangers lurked out there. That's what he'd told himself, anyway, that protecting them was his duty. But somewhere along the line, he'd realized duty didn't cover it.

Drawing in a painful breath, he could still smell her scent. He'd wanted to gather her lithe, little body in his arms to comfort her. He'd wanted to touch her soft skin and kiss away her fears.

Vehemently shaking his head, he shut the fantasy out of his mind. What was wrong with him? She was his friend's wife. Corry was the only one who could kiss away her fears. And Corry was dead.

Chapter Two

Lying in his bed, Justin stared into the darkness and swiped angrily at his tears. He was too old to cry. Only girls and babies cried. Dad wouldn't be proud of him if he cried. Of course, Dad wouldn't be proud of him for breaking into Harper's store tonight, either.

But Dad was gone. He'd left him here to deal with things on his own. And he was tired of being teased, of being called a wuss.

He had to do tough things to get the guys to respect him, especially being the shrimp he was. And Rick and Pete had said they needed his help tonight. What was he gonna do, tell them his mother wouldn't let him go out after nine? Yeah, right.

He stroked Sheba and sucked in a guilty breath. Upsetting Mom was another thing Dad wouldn't be proud of him for. But how'd he know David would happen to drive by and see them in the alley? It was David's fault Mom had to ever find out.

Everything was David's fault. He didn't know squat. If he did, he would have made sure Dad didn't get shot. But he hadn't. He'd let Dad take the bullet, and he knew it. That's why he hadn't bothered to stop by since that night.

Well, David better not give him too much grief. Because Justin had his number.

After school the next day, Nan waited inside Harper's drugstore door, her dress and pantyhose clinging to her damp body. The small fan whirring inadequately down one narrow aisle in the cluttered store did nothing to alleviate the trapped heat. The musty odor of old wood blended with medicinal smells teased a sneeze from her.

Justin shuffled up the crowded aisle to the counter in the front of the store where Mr. Harper leaned on his cane, his white head bobbing, his spectacles hovering on the end of his hawk-like nose.

"What can I do for you, Justin?"

"Uh, my mom says I have to apologize."

She could barely hear his words. After discarding the idea of grounding him until he grew up, she'd decided the best way to stir his dormant conscience was to make him face Mr. Harper and try to work out a way to repay him.

"Apologize?" The old man's crackly voice sliced the heavy air.

Justin cleared his throat. "I'm sorry I broke your window last night, and my mom says I have to ask you for a job to pay for it."

Nan held her breath, searching for a sign her son's admission was stirring his conscience.

A wrinkled scowl replaced the old man's smile. "*You* are the hoodlum who's been breaking my windows?"

Her heart lurched. He'd broken others?

Justin's slight body tensing, he threw back his shoulders and stared up at the old man. "Wait a minute. The only window I broke was the one in the alley last night."

Mr. Harper's ancient face turned red. "You young outlaw. You know very well this is the third one I've had to replace this summer."

"Well, I didn't break the others."

This was not going well. If Justin broke all those windows, she'd make sure he paid for them, but what if he hadn't? Being falsely accused would only make things worse.

Mr. Harper shook his head. "You ought to be ashamed. Windows cost a lot of money."

"I'm telling the truth. But why listen to a kid?" Justin's voice rang with insolence.

She'd better jump in before this whole thing got out of hand. She charged up the aisle. "Did you break those windows, Justin?"

Her son turned to her, a scowl on his face. "No, I didn't. Just last night."

She peered into his gray eyes, trying to determine

whether or not he was lying. She couldn't be sure. All she knew was she wanted desperately to believe he wouldn't lie to her.

Mr. Harper's expression spoke of anything but kindness. "Maybe you caught him only once, but I've had three windows broken. Those windows cost fifty dollars apiece. I'd say you owe me $150."

She stared in astonishment at the old man's angry face. Where in the world would she come up with $150? "My son will pay for the window he broke, but you can't hold him responsible for the others if he says he didn't break them."

"I've filed police reports every time. We'll see what the police have to say about who's responsible."

She had trouble catching her breath. "Be reasonable, Mr. Harper."

"Reasonable? That's the trouble with kids these days. Parents think their kids can do nothing wrong. Nobody takes responsibility."

Disbelief shot through her. "You know our family. We want to do the right thing. That's why Justin and I are here. But I don't think you should assume he's lying."

"One hundred and fifty dollars," Mr. Harper said with finality.

Hot anger flooded her. What a bitter old man. A ghostly visit from his past probably wouldn't even faze him. She grasped her son's hand and turned to leave. "Come on, Justin. We're finished here."

Outside the store, Nan bit her lip to keep from

spouting her anger. She wanted to scream at some-body. Instead, she blindly strode to her car.

Justin shuffled at her side, his shoulders hunched. "See, Mom. You can't admit anything. People are just waiting to nail you."

She glared at him. "Don't," she snapped. How could an eleven-year-old have such a cynical view of life? And what happened to his conscience? His attitude scared her to death. "You can't blame Mr. Harper for not trusting you. You broke the law."

"No big deal."

Stunned, she peered at her son as if he were a stranger. "Where did you ever get the idea that breaking the law is no big deal?"

He shrugged. "We're just kids, Mom. No guns. No nothing. Just kids. And the cops have better things to do than deal with kids."

She glared at him. He sounded so hard, so cynical. Fear shivered through her. They reached the car and climbed in, and she turned to him. "I have to ask you. Did you break the other windows? Or know anything about them?"

Justin shook his head, but he couldn't meet her eyes. "I swear, Mom."

Her son was lying to her. Stifling the panic screaming in her ears, she started the car and zoomed away from the curb. "You'll have to pay Mr. Harper for the windows. I'm holding you personally responsible."

He stared at her like she'd lost her mind. "How am I going to earn a hundred and fifty bucks?"

"You'll work for it, that's how."

"Who's gonna give me a job? I'm a kid."

Who indeed? Certainly not Mr. Harper. She'd been naive to hope he might let Justin work in the drugstore. "You'd better put your thinking cap on."

Justin scowled, his chin jutting.

"In the meantime, I'm grounding you until further notice." Grounding him fell far short of solving his problems, but she'd done everything she knew to do. Family counseling, a psychologist, the Big Brother program. Nothing had worked. This situation was beyond her control. Justin was in crisis, and he needed help she couldn't provide by herself.

David had offered that help.

But what if Justin began to rely on David too much? What if he became emotionally dependent on him? David was a sheriff's deputy, for heaven's sake. Like Justin's father, who'd been killed in the line of duty.

But right now, Justin becoming emotionally dependent on David seemed less frightening than failing to get the help her son needed.

The sun hot on his shoulders, David sat in a deck chair in his swim trunks, cradling the portable phone to his neck and listening to the ringing on the other end. When he'd listened to Nan's message on his answering machine, she'd sounded worried.

"Marshall Field's at Hilldale. How may I help you?" An unfamiliar voice, ringing with efficiency, spoke into his ear.

He frowned and squinted at the notepad balanced

on his knee. Had he punched in the right number?
"Uh, I'd like to speak to Nan Kramer."

"One moment. Please stay on the line until someone picks up in the Children's Department." An im-
mediate click told him he didn't have to respond.
Watching languid waves lap the shoreline, he worked
at the caulk lodged around his fingernails from chink-
ing his log house all morning and listened to an insipid
arrangement of "Send in the Clowns" on the tele-
phone.

"Children's wear. May I help you?" Nan's soft
voice answered.

He snapped to full attention. "Nan? It's David."

"Thank you for returning my call. I'm afraid the
problem is even worse than we thought." The worry
in her voice made him sick inside.

What else had Justin gotten into? "What do you
mean?"

"I can't talk now. Every mother in the area is stock-
ing up on school clothes today. But I'm interested in
listening to your ideas. Could you come over tonight
after the kids are in bed? I don't want them listening
in."

He clenched his jaw. When he'd finally crawled into
bed after waiting until dawn for her to turn out her
light, he'd dreamed of sitting in her cozy living room
with her late at night with the kids tucked in. Trouble
was, in his dream, he'd ended up making love to her
on her living room floor. He was one mixed-up deputy, that was for sure. Shaking his head, he raked his
fingers through his hair. "Uh, I can't do that."

"Oh."

The disappointment in that one little word pierced him painfully. He cared too much to let his confused libido keep him from seeing her. She was a beautiful woman, so he'd dreamed about her. What was surprising about that? Still… "I can meet you earlier, if that works."

"I get off work a little after five. Can you be at the Upstairs Downstairs Deli in Hilldale?"

"Sure." He opened his eyes, hoping he could find the deli without searching the entire mall.

"It's right in front, across from the bookstore. You can't miss it."

He frowned. She must have read his mind. "Great. See you then."

"Thank you, David."

"No need—" The line went dead. Nan's gentle smile vivid in his imagination, he absently clicked off the phone and set it on the nearby table as he climbed to his feet. He checked his watch and strode for the lakeshore. He had two good hours before he needed to get cleaned up to meet her, and swimming always helped him straighten things out in his mind.

He sprinted into the lake, the water jolting as it enveloped his legs. Diving under, his body sliced the cold, murky silence until his lungs pounded for air.

David scrunched his long legs under a table at the deli and watched for Nan. The subtle clink of dishes mingled with the murmur of conversation as more tables filled. The mouthwatering aroma of cooking food made his stomach growl with interest. He couldn't remember eating today.

Sipping ice water, he tried to ignore the smile the waitress tossed his way every time she hustled by. He'd told her he was meeting a friend, and she persisted in flirting anyway. Apparently, she'd assumed his friend was male.

He spotted Nan.

She floated up the few steps to the dining room, pausing to answer the waitress's greeting. Nan's deep-blue dress skimmed her supple body and stopped just below her knees to reveal her trim legs, muscles taut in black, high-heeled shoes.

Adrenaline shot through him as the intimacy of his dream pervaded his senses. He had to get that dream out of his mind and concentrate on Justin. He took a guilty gulp of ice water.

The waitress pointed in his direction. Nan's golden head turned, a warm smile lit her face and she glided toward him.

Returning her smile, he lunged out of the booth, hitting his knee on the corner of the table. Pain shot down into his shin while he tried not to notice.

"Hi," she said.

He nodded.

She sat down, and he lowered himself into the booth, jamming his legs under the tiny table again. He'd made a mistake. He should have met her in a park, someplace he could move around. Sitting was something he never did well.

"May I take your order now?" The waitress grinned down at him.

He looked at Nan. The neckline of her blue dress was scooped, revealing creamy skin. He dragged his gaze to her face. Her intense deep-blue eyes jolted him, eyes the color of the sea. What the hell was wrong with him? He focused on the lively floral pattern of the booth behind her.

"I'd like an iced tea, please."

Realizing food no longer interested him, he finally found his voice. "Two iced teas."

The waitress left again.

"It's still a beautiful day out there," Nan ventured. "I work upstairs with air-conditioning and no windows. I never know what the weather is doing."

"How often do you work?" A somewhat intelligent question.

"Four days during the week, now that Brenda's in kindergarten. I need time with the kids on weekends. Anyway, an all-day sitter would cost more than I'd make."

The shadows under her eyes worried him. And why wouldn't she have shadows under her eyes with her heavy load? Being both mother and father to three active kids had to be grueling. He cast around for something else to say. "Susan Gardner told me you're taking classes at the university."

She smiled. "Six credits. I'm taking basic education classes two very long evenings a week. Maybe I'll earn a degree by the time I'm fifty." Amusement lit her eyes.

She still had her droll, little sense of humor. He remembered her teasing him about his willpower when he'd never dated more than once or twice the friends she'd fixed him up with. But she'd known his willpower had nothing to do with it. He hadn't made a secret of the fact that he never planned to marry. Or that by dating a woman only once or twice, he avoided complications and expectations. Nan had teased him about that, too.

"You look as if you're working out a significant problem, David."

"I'm sorry. I have a lot on my mind." An understatement if he'd ever made one. What had they been talking about? Oh yeah. About her classes at the university. "Do you ever do anything fun?"

She gave him a quizzical frown. "My classes are fun. And the kids and I swim and picnic and bike."

"You look pale. You were always tanned in the summers." Now he sounded critical.

"I don't get outside as often as I'd like. There's so little time. But the kids and I do something fun most weekends."

The kids. Justin. That's what they needed to talk about. "What's happening with Justin?"

Her smile fading, she slumped as though a heavy weight descended on her. "He's playing tough guy. He won't even admit he's done anything wrong. I took him to apologize to Mr. Harper, and the man was irate. This is his *third* broken window this summer."

David heaved a sigh. "Did Justin admit to breaking the others?"

The waitress arrived with iced tea. Nan and David stared at the table and waited until she left.

Plucking a slice of lemon from its perch on his glass, he laid it on his napkin.

Nan daintily squeezed her slice of lemon into her tea. "Justin said he didn't break the others. But he's lying about something. Even if he didn't break them, he knows something about it." She raised her gaze to meet his. "Justin believes the police are too busy to worry about kids." She paused as though waiting for him to disagree with her son's judgment.

He wished he could. "Too many kids fall through the cracks until their crimes become serious enough to warrant the time it takes to prosecute." By then it was often too late to save the kid. He couldn't let that happen to Corry's boy. And Nan's. Her kids were everything to her. He had to turn Justin around before he got into bigger trouble. He owed Corry.

"Justin's cynicism really frightens me." Fear shone from her eyes, along with the worry and the exhaustion.

"It's important he take responsibility for his actions. Do you know his friends?"

She shook her head. "He never invites anyone over. When I press him to bring somebody along on a family outing, he gets angry. Either he doesn't have any friends, or he thinks I'll disapprove of them."

A familiar story. But how many troubled kids had a devoted mother like Nan? In all the times he'd seen her with them, she'd been tireless in caring for their needs. Guiding, teaching, encouraging them to explore with lots of hugs and smiles and fun. A vision of her in her conservative blue swimsuit, making a game of slathering sunscreen on a giggling Justin filled David's mind.

Her soft lips puckered around the rim of her glass as she sipped the tea.

He lowered his eyes to the table and played with his spoon while he tried to focus on the subject at hand.

"Will Justin be punished in some way?" Nan asked.

"Punishment will be up to you. He's a juvenile, and you said last night he hasn't been in trouble before. How do you plan to discipline him?"

Her chin lifted slightly. "I've told him he has to pay for the broken windows."

"Good."

"And I grounded him until further notice." Clamping her lips in a firm line, she punctuated her announcement with a decisive nod.

David smiled. She looked so determined. In the time he'd known her, he'd learned she could carry off anything she set her mind to. But did she have that same fortitude when it came to disciplining her son? "Are you as tough with Justin as you sound?"

"What do you mean?"

"Do you stick to your guns with him?"

Her eyes flashed with indignation. "I know how to deal with my children. But Justin requires help I can't provide."

He chucked his smile. He hadn't meant to offend her. "I didn't mean—Nan, you're a great mom."

She waved away his compliment. "Last night you said it's hard for a boy to learn how to become a man without a father to teach him. You grew up without a father, didn't you?"

He thought about sedate and boring Joe Demming, whose idea of parenting had been to buy a television set for David's room so he'd spend more time in there, sitting quietly. He'd never used it. As a result, his stepfather was convinced David was ungrateful, which had justified the man's contempt for anything David ever did. "I had a stepfather who preferred to believe I didn't exist."

She sipped the tea, her vivid-blue eyes conveying sympathy and concern over her glass. "How did you turn out to be such an upstanding, law-abiding citizen?"

He grinned. "I took my share of detours along the way before Milt Adams, my high school principal, laid down the law and made it stick. He'd take groups of troubled kids camping and backpacking on weekends, and we learned in a hurry we weren't so tough. And how relying on others was sometimes necessary."

"Is that what you think Justin needs to learn?"

"Yeah, that and to take responsibility for his actions. At-risk kids need to stop blaming the system or other people for their problems. They need to learn *they're* responsible for making something out of their lives."

She drew in a long, deep breath. "How long do you work with the boys?"

"For the first six months we're pretty intense. After that, we get the group together once a month. Otherwise, it's up to the kids. They call us when they have a problem or when they can't handle something that happens to them."

"Who do you work with?"

"Cindy Manning. She's a social worker who happens to be married to my partner. I put in long hours with the department, so I won't be able to personally supervise Justin all the time. And it's better for the kids to learn to deal with both Cindy and me. That way, one of us should always be available."

She studied her glass of tea. "My big worry is that Justin could become emotionally dependent on you. And if something happened to you…" She met his eyes, a plea for understanding obvious.

His heart swelled with admiration and respect. Under her gentle femininity, she had more common sense and courage than any woman he'd ever met. Of course she'd worry about Justin placing his trust in another deputy. She wouldn't be the parent he knew she was if she didn't worry about that. "That's a concern for me, too. I have to form a bond with him to win his trust, but I don't encourage dependence in any of the kids. My aim is to help Justin, not to replace his father. Nobody can do that. Not ever."

She nodded, shadows dimming the deep blue pools of her eyes. "Will you come to supper tomorrow and talk to Justin?"

Supper at Nan's house had a nice ring to it, and it would give him the perfect opportunity to begin to establish a rapport with Justin. Remembering his dream, he reconsidered. Nan's house, the kids tucked in for the night? Probably not the best idea. "I have to work," he fibbed.

"Oh." A tiny frown crinkled the corners of her eyes.

"I'll look at my schedule and figure out a time to meet with him." Feeling like a heel, he flexed his fingers and clenched them around his glass of iced tea, then downed the whole thing without tasting it.

A few minutes later he was walking with Nan to the parking lot, listening to the soft rustle of her dress as she moved, the staccato click of her high heels on the asphalt, noting the scent of her perfume—all kept his mind filled with the memory of his dream and inspired thoughts of touching her.

He finally relented enough to allow his fingers to clasp her elbow to guide her through the maze of automobiles to her little blue Toyota.

She unlocked the door, then turned and laid her hand on his arm, the gold band on her ring finger catching the sun's rays.

"You still wear your wedding ring." He wondered why that surprised him.

She followed his gaze, her features softening as she looked at the ring. "I've never thought about taking it off." She raised her gaze to meet his, calm acceptance in her eyes. "Corry was my life partner. I don't know how else to explain it."

She talked as if her life was over, but she was too young to give up on life. "Are you happy alone?" he asked quietly.

She sighed. "My children don't need any more emotional upheaval. All I want is to raise them in peace." Her eyes filled with remembered pain. "It's taken me quite a while to get to this place."

Her pain tormented him. If only Corry were here to take her in his arms right now and make her pain go away. But, of course, he wasn't. If only David had charged into the alley first that fatal night. But he hadn't. If only he'd been there for Nan through the aftermath. But he hadn't done that, either. He clenched his teeth until the throb in his jaw reminded him to let up. He desperately wanted to slam his fist into something.

She grasped his hand firmly. "You need to let the anger go. Along with all that guilt you're carrying around."

Her skin was warm and silky smooth, and her touch soothed like a healing balm. In her eyes he saw only warmth and concern and approval. No blame, not even a hint of it. No remorse that he was standing here with her instead of her husband.

He cleared his throat and rallied his defenses. "I've been trying hard to do that."

"I know it isn't easy, but if you let the anger consume you, you can't heal."

He nodded. "Like Justin?"

She sighed. "Yes, like Justin. If I can get him on the right track…"

"Now that's something I can help you with." He gave her hand a confident squeeze.

She smiled into his eyes. "I believe you can."

He drew in a deep breath of clean air. Her faith in him swept away a little of the guilt that had weighed him down since Corry's death. "Will you get some sleep tonight and try not to worry so much?"

She gave him a puzzled little frown. "Do I look haggard?"

He shook his head. "No, you look tired. And worried."

She gave a little laugh. "So diplomatically put."

He grinned into her clear, blue eyes, delighted he'd made her laugh. But making her laugh wasn't enough. She needed more than that. She needed concrete help with her son. He reached around her and opened her car door. "What time do you want me for dinner tomorrow night?"

She looked up at him as she ducked into the car, her eyes widening in surprise. "You said you had to work."

Oh yeah, that's what he'd said all right. "Uh, I'll get somebody to cover for me," he fibbed. "Getting started with Justin is important."

"Terrific. How about six-thirty?"

"Six-thirty is fine." He slammed her door shut and stepped back.

Her Toyota purred to life. She rolled down the window. "As I recall, you like lasagna."

"I love your lasagna."

She smiled and drove off.

He waved as she sped away, then strode to his Jeep, climbed in and tore out of the parking lot. She'd taken him up on his offer to guide Justin through this difficult time, and he'd be damned if he'd let her down.

Hell, no need to be so worried about that dream. She still wore her wedding ring, for crying out loud. She wasn't any more available than she'd ever been.

Chapter Three

"One fork or two?" Melody slammed cupboard doors, collecting dishes, silverware and the red checkered tablecloth to set the table on the screened porch.

"Two forks," Nan decided, glancing at her watch. Almost six-thirty. David would arrive soon. Hopefully, he wouldn't be put off by Justin's lack of enthusiasm. He'd probably worked with kids every bit as negative as her son. It was just that so much depended on whether or not he could get Justin to cooperate. It was her one hope to get their lives back to normal.

"Should I put cups on the table?" Melody asked.

"Set them on the counter for later. I'll serve iced coffee with dessert." Tearing lettuce into a salad bowl, Nan swiped the back of her hand across her forehead. Heat from the oven had turned the kitchen into a sauna. If she'd known the temperature would climb into the mideighties today, she wouldn't have promised David lasagna.

"What's for dessert?" Justin asked, filling the water pitcher with ice.

"The cherry cream recipe Daddy always loved. I served it one time when David stayed for supper. I think he liked it."

"I don't like cherries," Justin grumbled.

She gave her son an apologetic look.

"Cherries?" Brenda puckered her little mouth.

"Not sour ones, Brenda." Donning her oven mitts, Nan swept the oven door open, took out the giant pan of bubbling lasagna and set it on the wood cutting board. The aroma wafted through the room along with more steam. Retrieving tomatoes and a bell pepper from the refrigerator, she lingered in front of the open door to absorb the cool air.

The doorbell startled her. Her three children stopped in their tracks and stared at her. Obviously, they'd picked up on her nervous tension.

"I'll get it." Melody darted around the kitchen table.

"No, Melody. I want Justin to answer the door." Nan sliced the tomatoes with far more urgency than the task required. She had to calm down. Sheer will on her part would not ensure her son's cooperation.

Justin glared at her. "I don't know what to say to him."

"Hi would be good," Nan suggested. "Then let him in and bring him to the kitchen."

Justin scowled, set the full water pitcher on the counter with a thud and sauntered out of the room.

Nan closed her eyes and dragged in a breath of patience. Justin's demeanor didn't leave too much room to hope he'd cooperate with David, but giving him another lecture probably wouldn't help, either.

"I don't know why I couldn't answer the door," Melody complained. "David is my guest, too, isn't he?"

"Of course he is. But you already feel comfortable greeting people at the door. Justin needs to learn how." Nan finished slicing the tomatoes into the salad.

"So now he *always* gets to answer the door?"

Pausing, she sighed and focused on her daughter. "No, Melody. Not always. But we never have a male guest, so this is a good time to let Justin do it."

Melody seemed satisfied. At least, she appeared to run out of complaints for the moment.

Nan resumed chopping.

"David brought ice cream," Justin announced without a bit of enthusiasm.

"I remembered the kids used to like butter brickle, but Justin says he doesn't like it anymore." David's rich baritone seemed unperturbed by Justin's rejection.

Nan briefly closed her eyes. Justin loved butter brickle ice cream. With a sigh, she finished tossing the salad. "That was very thoughtful, David."

Melody hustled forward. "Well, I like it. I'll put it in the freezer before it melts."

"I like it, too," Brenda piped up.

Drying her hands with a paper towel, Nan turned to face their guest.

He filled the doorway, a hesitant smile in his chocolate eyes. A white knit shirt stretched across his broad chest and gave her a glimpse of dark chest hair at the open throat. He wore denim shorts, his long, bronze legs ending in sockless Nikes. An Adonis. She blinked, but she couldn't stop staring.

He frowned. "Am I early?"

She shook her head. She'd seen him in street clothes before, as recently as yesterday at the deli. And he'd looked terrific. But standing in her kitchen, he seemed so big and strong and male.

"What's wrong, Mom?" Melody asked.

Drawing in a deep breath, Nan pulled her gaze from David and fought for reason. "I'm fine. I think it's the heat." She tried to laugh.

"It must be a hundred degrees in here." Leaning forward, he looked ready to catch her in case she fainted.

She'd rather die than faint. "The oven," she said weakly, focusing on the floor.

"I should have insisted on grilling burgers in this heat. I never thought about lasagna needing baking." He shook his head as if he couldn't believe he'd made such a blunder.

Now he felt guilty. Not a very good start to the evening. What in the world was wrong with her? This reaction to David was anything but normal. Turning to the pitcher of ice water on the counter, she filled a glass and gulped half of it.

Silence hung in the room while everybody waited for her to pull herself together.

"That lasagna smells wonderful. I could smell it all the way up the sidewalk," David said.

Fussing with the salad, Nan marveled at the sexy resonance of his deep baritone. What in the world was going on? This was David, for heaven's sake. Corry's and her friend. And she was Nan Kramer, mother of three, who had supper to get on the table. "I hope you brought your appetite. It's cooler on the porch, so we'll eat out there. Justin, take the water pitcher and show David the way. Melody, take the salad; Brenda, the rolls."

"I'll get the lasagna." David strode to the counter, grabbed the oven mitts and hefted the large pan. "Lead the way. I'm right behind you. Good thing you made a lot of this because I'm starved."

They all trooped onto the porch and settled themselves at the table, the cooler temperature a welcome relief. David positioned himself between Justin and Melody, across the table from Nan and Brenda.

"The pan is too hot to pass around. If you hand me your plate, I'll serve the lasagna." Nan extended her hand to David, trying hard to keep it steady. If he noticed it was shaking, he'd think for sure she was suffering from heat stroke. "Justin, please pour water for everyone."

Before long, everyone was served, and the children were eating quietly, stiffly observant of their guest.

David peered across the table at her with appreciation in his eyes. "This is delicious. I've missed your great cooking."

She smiled, way too pleased by his simple compliment. "Thank you."

He'd said he was starved, and he ate enthusiastically enough to back up his words.

She knew, because she couldn't seem to stop her eyes from stealing glances. She'd forgotten his strong jawline and the cleft in his chin. And the way the corners of his mouth turned up when he smiled. But when had she become a connoisseur of attractive men? She'd laugh at herself if she wasn't so darn off balance and fluttery.

"Where do you live?" Brenda took it upon herself to get a conversation going.

"I live near Lake Mendota. Not far from your house."

Nan raised an eyebrow. "When did you move out of Madison?"

David met her gaze. "Not long after you did, actually." Something flickered in his eyes, something she couldn't identify.

"Do you still have a boat?" Melody asked.

"I sure do. I bought a new runabout this summer."

"Is Runabout your boat's name?" Justin's interest seemed piqued, a hopeful sign.

"I named her the *Solo*. A runabout is a type of boat. Among other things, she has enough speed for water-skiing." He glanced at Nan. "Your mother's sport."

Nan shot him a doubtful look. They used to water-ski many summer days, and she'd loved it, but it seemed so long ago. "I probably couldn't even get up on skis anymore."

"I think it's kind of like riding a bike. You don't forget. Especially at the level you ski."

She'd never been freer than when she'd skimmed across the water, the wind and spray whipping her body, the speed filling her with adrenaline. Often, Corry or David skied at her side while the other operated the boat. So long ago. Back when she'd taken security and normal family life for granted.

"I got up on skis once." Melody reclaimed her hold on David's attention.

"I remember," David said. "You got up in two tries, and you were only eight years old."

Melody's eyes widened in pleasure.

Nan smiled. She'd watched Melody's triumph from shore, holding tiny Brenda in her arms. Now David's sensitivity with her teenage daughter warmed Nan's heart. He seemed to sense Melody's fragile self-confidence.

"Do you think I could try again sometime?"

"Melody." Nan shot David an apologetic look. She should have stepped in before her daughter put him on the spot.

"I'm sure we can arrange that, Melody. If it's okay with your mom." David peered at Nan.

Everybody at the table looked expectantly at her.

But she couldn't bring herself to agree. For one thing, her daughter had wheedled the invitation. And for another, she strove to err on the side of caution where her children's safety was concerned. "We'll see."

"Please, Mom. We never do anything exciting," Melody chirped.

Nan frowned a warning at her tenacious daughter.

David raised his dark brows and worried his bottom lip. He looked more amused than anything else. "Some weekend when I'm off work, it would be fun."

Nan shifted uncomfortably. "You're not helping."

"Sorry."

Too late. She'd already caught the twinkle in his eyes, and if he was trying to look contrite, he was failing miserably.

"Can I go, too?" Brenda asked.

"You're too little to water-ski," Nan answered.

"I can watch." Anticipation shone in Brenda's big, gray eyes.

"Please, Mom," Melody and Brenda whined in unison.

Clearly it was one of those times Nan wished a hole would open in the floor and swallow her, along with her obnoxious kids. "We'll see." Her ambiguous reply produced expected slumps of disgust in her daughters. "We'll talk more about it later. Right now, Justin and Melody can clear the table and Brenda can help me with dessert."

"What job does David get?" Brenda asked, climbing out of her chair.

"Yeah. What job do I get?" David stood up, ready for action. Tall and muscular and virile.

Heat crept up her neck. Virile? What was she thinking? She cast around in her befuddled mind for a task for him to do. "You want to pour the iced coffee?"

He nodded, grinning his lopsided grin. "Lead me to it."

She grinned, totally unable to squelch her whole-hearted delight. And why shouldn't she be delighted? This evening was turning out better than she'd dared hope. It hadn't taken the girls long to relax with David. Even Justin seemed resigned to accepting David's presence. Who knew? Maybe he'd even cooperate. "We have cherry cream dessert and the ice cream David brought. Name your preference."

"Ice cream," the girls said in unison.

"The cherry stuff," Justin grumped.

Frustration slid through Nan. Justin had chosen the dessert he didn't like over the ice cream he loved, obviously because the ice cream was David's offering. She sure hoped David could get past Justin's attitude.

While the two older kids set about the flutter of clearing the table, Brenda and David followed Nan into the kitchen where David proved to be a more than competent helper. He accepted Brenda's instructions with good-natured diligence, which thrilled the five-year-old.

Seated at the table again facing their desserts, everyone dug in. Nan listened to her children's banter with half an ear and noticed the way David's eyes crinkled in curiosity and amusement as he watched them.

She'd always known he loved kids. He'd won her over early on with his unabashed absorption in Brenda's first smile, her first tooth, her first steps. He'd been almost as proud as Corry had been. It was so good to have David back in their lives again.

But her visceral awareness of him wasn't something she'd experienced before. Everything he did reminded her she was a woman. That she had her own needs. Needs she'd blocked out the past two years. Needs she'd just as soon block out for the rest of her life because she had no intention of doing anything about them. She would always be Corry's wife—period.

"Justin's practically a celebrity at school. And I, his own sister, had to hear the news from Rachel Piddington, of all people. I've never been so mortified in my life." Melody jammed a spoonful of ice cream into her mouth.

Nan stopped chewing and frowned at her daughter.

"Shut up, Mel." Justin peered around David and glared at his sister. "You're not supposed to tattle while we eat. It's bad for indigestion."

"Bad for digestion, you idiot. Anyway, we're almost done eating. Justin's practically a hero because he didn't turn Rick Kellogg and Pete Delaney over to the police that night."

Nan drew in a quick breath at Melody's words.

"Shut up." Justin jumped up from his chair.

Oh, for heaven's sake. Now she had a family crisis on her hands. "Sit down, Justin. If the kids at school know, it's not a secret anymore." She glanced at David.

He shot her a look of pure calm.

Justin plunked into his chair, his spine stiff.

Melody continued her story. "Rick told Rachel he

waited half the night for the police to come to his house, but no one showed up. He couldn't believe Justin would keep his mouth shut.''

"Mom," Justin yelled. "Make Melody shut up." He glowered at Nan, his face flushed with anger.

"I, for one, am very interested in Melody's story," David said matter-of-factly.

Nan cringed. Did he know what he was doing? How would he gain Justin's cooperation if he alienated him?

Melody turned to David. "You'd think somebody would have mentioned the police were at our house. Nobody tells me anything around here."

Brenda frowned at her brother. "The police? What did you do, Justin? Be a hero?"

Melody snorted in disgust. "He's not a hero, Bren. Only retards like Rick and Pete think so."

"Melody's right," Nan said. "Justin is not a hero. He and his friends broke a window in Mr. Harper's store."

Brenda turned to Justin, her eyes as big as saucers. "Was it a accident?"

Justin shook his head.

Brenda's little forehead puckered. "Oh, Justin. Did you forget it was a bad thing?"

Justin scowled at his little sister.

Nan held her breath. Brenda idolized her brother, and he couldn't seem to come up with one of his flip answers for her. At least he cared what *she* thought.

"I didn't forget, Bren. I guess I wasn't thinking straight," Justin admitted.

Brenda nodded as though she understood perfectly.

Justin's honesty and Brenda's total acceptance hit Nan like a kick in the stomach. He used to open up to her that way. Before Corry died. Before fear and insecurity pervaded their little family. A hush settled over everyone at the table. Even Melody was silent.

"Will you have to go to jail?" Brenda asked.

Justin shook his head. "Kids don't go to jail."

The little girl frowned, a puzzled expression on her face.

"Justin hasn't gotten into trouble before," David explained. "So his family is responsible for his punishment."

Nan nodded. "And we have to make sure he doesn't get into trouble again."

"Me, too?" Brenda piped up.

David grinned. "You too, peanut."

A pain stabbed Nan's heart. Peanut was Corry's nickname for Brenda. Nan dabbed shakily at her lips with her napkin, relieved David's attention centered on her children. She reached for her cup of iced coffee. Melody's timing couldn't have been worse. Justin looked so angry, and just when he was letting down his guard around David. But she couldn't blame her daughter for expressing resentment that she hadn't been told what was going on in her own family.

She had meant to tell Melody what had happened, but last evening had been hectic with Scouts and church choir. And when they'd gotten home, homework had claimed everyone's attention until bedtime.

David laid his napkin on the table beside his coffee cup. "Justin, why don't you show me the backyard?"

"That's a good idea." Nan tried to sound enthusiastic but probably didn't succeed.

Glowering at her, Justin heaved a sigh and slid back his chair with a screech. He looked as if he faced the guillotine.

Nan bit her lip and glanced at David.

He gave her an encouraging wink. "Will you join us in a little while?"

She nodded, the wink not doing too much to reassure her.

"I'm really looking forward to waterskiing, David." Melody had to get in one last pitch.

"As soon as your mother gives the word." David closed the door behind Justin and himself and followed the reluctant boy into the yard.

Nan breathed a little prayer that David could get through Justin's negativity. While the girls cleared the table and stacked the dishes for later, Nan stored the leftovers in containers and wondered what was going on in the backyard.

"He's so *nice*." Melody beamed, rinsing the dishes and staring out the window above the sink.

"Yes, he is." Nan walked over and stood at her daughter's side to share her view of the backyard. David and Justin perched on idle swings in Brenda's swing set, David talking, his long legs stretched in front of him near ground level. Justin soberly nodded a couple of times. At least, it looked as if he might be listening.

"Isn't David handsome, Mom?"

Nan noted Melody's beaming expression and nodded. What woman in her right mind wouldn't think so? Probably he elicited admiration in every female, no matter what age. Married or not. Maybe her own response to him was only natural.

"Can I go outside now, Mommy?" Brenda stood in the doorway, poised for flight.

Melody dried her hands with a dish towel. "I'll go with you."

"Not now, girls. David needs to talk to Justin. I picked up *Little Women* at the library today. It's in my book bag by the couch." The video was a little mature for Brenda, but Melody watched *Bambi* last time. It was one of the trade-offs with the eight-year gap in their ages.

"It's not fair," Melody grumbled. "Come on, Bren."

Nan headed down the hall to the bathroom to freshen up. She ran a brush through her hair, applied lip gloss and dabbed her flushed cheeks with a splash of cool water.

Refreshed, she checked the view of the backyard from the kitchen window again. David and Justin still sat on the swings, Justin's expression not enthusiastic but not defiant, either.

She closed the screen door behind her and welcomed the evening air. The smell of charcoal from neighbors' grills hung in the humidity. Dusk settling, her backyard took on the soft haze of summer's end when each hour outdoors is more precious because of

its limited supply. Children's voices rang from somewhere down the street. She strolled over to the swing
set.

David watched her approach, his lips curving into
a smile.

Strangely self-conscious, she returned his smile,
then focused on Justin. Although he didn't wear a
smile, his chin wasn't jutting. Things couldn't have
gone too badly.

"We're working out Justin's contract."

"David's gonna hire me to work for him so I can
earn money to pay for the window. And he's gonna
talk to Harper."

"Mr. Harper," she corrected automatically. "Do
you have work for him, David?"

"I have plenty of odd jobs I never have time to do.
The way I see it, if he works with Cindy and me and
pays for the window he broke, that should take care
of it."

Justin nodded agreeably.

Hope winged into her heart. David had actually gotten Justin's cooperation. Wonders never ceased.

Sheba bounded from the bushes near the swings and
brushed back and forth against Nan's legs. She bent
and stroked the cat's silky coat.

"If it's okay with you, Justin says he'd like to go
out on the *Solo* with me tomorrow morning." David
peered at her, waiting for her answer.

A flutter of fear for Justin's safety crept through her.
She dismissed it. Of course David would make sure
her son was safe. And although Justin kept his ex-

pression guarded, she detected an interest she hadn't seen for a very long time.

A pang settled near her heart. She missed her little boy with golden curls whose energetic antics and infectious laugh could light up her most stressful day. She wanted him back. "It sounds like fun."

"Good. Justin, I'll pick you up about seven tomorrow morning. That way we can get out on the water before the weekend crowd. Okay?"

"Yeah. Are we done?"

David gave him a nod.

Justin climbed off the swing, swooped Sheba into his arms and shuffled across the lawn to the house.

Nan turned to David. "How did you get him to cooperate?"

David grinned. "I outlined his options, and he chose the least offensive one. I think a combination of counseling and work will suit him well."

She steadied the swing and sat down. "He can be stubborn, especially when he senses someone is trying to help him. And after Melody made him so angry, I worried you didn't have a chance."

"He told me he didn't break any windows before Wednesday night. I believe him, but I think you're right. He knows more than he's telling."

A dog barked somewhere in the distance. Insects hummed. Nan sensed a stillness settling between David and her. She felt so close to him. So secure. So safe. But she should let him off the hook on the outing Melody had wheedled out of him. "Don't feel obligated to take Melody skiing. I think you've cast a spell over all three of the kids." To say nothing of their mother.

His lips curved into a slow easy smile that relaxed his jawline and crinkled his eyes. "The kids are great. You're doing a fantastic job."

Her heart lurched, and tears stung her eyes. All her concern and frustration in trying to help Justin seemed to converge. "I've been so worried. You have no idea." Reaching out, she laid her hand on his forearm.

He tensed, his smile vanishing. "I should have been there for you and the kids after Corry died. Especially after everything he did for me." He covered her hand with his, his skin rough and hot.

He'd loved Corry, too. It couldn't be easy for him to be around her and the kids. "You're here now. Justin really needs you now."

"Nan, I..." Clasping her hand, he stood up and drew her up with him.

She walked into his arms, slipping her hands around his narrow waist and hugging him close. His strong arms wrapped around her, making her feel protected and feminine. Laying her head on his broad chest, she savored his warmth and caring and listened to the pounding of his heart. He smelled of sun and the outdoors, and his heat radiated a warm glow through her.

Becoming aware of the hard planes of his body, she felt her pulse and breathing accelerate. Long-dormant desire flickered to life and sparked through her. A vision of his broad, muscular chest with its bronze skin and dark silky hair popped into her mind. She wanted to slide her hands under his shirt and stroke his skin.

No. This couldn't be happening. Alarm sent her back, straining out of his arms.

Scowling at her as if she were a stranger, he swallowed hard. He must have sensed he'd stirred something in her beyond friendship. He closed his eyes.

She wanted to disappear. She'd missed feeling a man's arms around her so much. The strength. The warmth. The caring. She'd gotten carried away. She'd definitely surprised David. And herself. Embarrassment heated her cheeks.

"It's getting late." The huskiness in his voice alarmed her even more. "I'll say goodbye to the kids." He strode for the house.

She stood stunned and as embarrassed as she'd ever been in her life. What happened? One minute she'd been relieved their lives would get back to normal. The next...

When her wits returned, she jogged to catch up.

He held the screen door open for her, careful to maintain a safe distance. He wouldn't even look at her.

Speechless, she followed him through the house. What could she say?

"Good night, kids," he hailed from the front door. "I'll pick you up at seven tomorrow morning, Justin."

Variations of "bye David" drifted from the vicinity of the television.

David's eyes were dark, unreadable, he seemed to glower down at her. "Thank you for supper." With that, he turned and strode out the door.

She stayed rooted to the spot, remorse and guilt

sweeping through her. "I'm sorry," she stammered to the screen door.

He climbed into his Jeep and eased it out into the street.

She watched until the Jeep disappeared. She was trembling. One minute she'd had everything under control. The next, she'd...she'd...thrown herself at David.

"Why did he go so fast, Mommy? I wanted to show him my picher." Standing at her elbow, Brenda frowned up at her.

"Was he in a hurry?" Melody asked from the living room floor.

"I guess so."

"I drawed a picher of his boat." Brenda held up a red and orange paper for Nan to admire.

"It's very nice," she said without seeing. She locked the screen door. "Get into your pajamas, guys."

"But we're watching the movie," Melody complained.

Nan desperately needed a few minutes alone to sort out the emotions and sensations that had blindsided her with David. "Take a break. You can finish the movie after you're ready for bed."

She headed for the kitchen. Her fluttery uneasiness during supper had escalated to full-scale turmoil. Running hot water into the sink full of stacked dishes, she squirted in too much soap and started scrubbing.

The warmth David created in her probably had a lot to do with their mutual love for Corry and her gratitude for his help with Justin. But warmth had changed to something else tonight.

Of course, she'd always been aware of his masculinity. She'd been married, not dead. His vitality invited a woman to respond. But before tonight, she'd never been struck dumb by his presence nor delighted in watching him chew his food.

When had she become a love-starved widow who threw herself at her male friends? Strange that she'd had no warning. Male companionship hadn't interested her in the least. Apparently that had changed. She fingered her wedding ring in the soapy water, guilt creeping through her.

She'd had a good marriage. She had three wonderful children, two in the throes of puberty. She didn't have time to deal with her own raging hormones.

She didn't want a man in her life. And even if she did someday, it could never be a deputy. She couldn't live with the fear of never knowing if he'd walk in the door at the end of his shift or not. And putting her children in danger of losing another daddy would be unthinkable.

David's tires squealed around curves in the lake road as he sucked in the humid night air pummeling him from the open window. The memory of Nan's delicate little body pressing against him still had him on fire. He felt her arms around his waist hugging him closer, her head on his chest, her breasts burning into him. Her scent, her softness…

She was his partner's wife, for crying out loud. What happened to his loyalty to Corry?

He pulled the Jeep into his driveway and jumped out. Striding to the back of the house, he yanked his shirt over his head and threw it onto the deck. He left his shoes in the sand, jogged to the lake and plunged into the cold water. Shock registered. But he aimed for numb.

Diving under, he shot through the cold blackness.

Nan had made him feel so welcome, and he'd really enjoyed interacting with the kids. He'd totally let down his guard.

He surfaced and swam hard toward lights beckoning from the far shore. Not until his tired muscles threatened to cramp did he turn back. Trudging out of the water, he sank down in the sand and stared up at zillions of stars.

Her lonely vulnerability was so tempting. And her trust made him twelve feet tall. It made him want to take her in his arms and make everything safe for her.

But he had to be sure she hadn't misplaced her trust. He had to get her out of his mind. Out of his dreams.

If she ever decided she wanted a man in her life, she needed some nice safe guy who lived a careful life. One who could offer her security and be a father to her kids. And David could no more be that kind of guy than fly.

But the image of her with any other man was something he couldn't bring himself to think about.

Chapter Four

The *Solo* slowed. Justin at the helm, David sat next to him in his black swim trunks, his aching muscles reminding him of his sleepless night on the beach. The sun might be shining brightly overhead, but fog clouded his tired mind.

Justin put the boat's engine in neutral and smoothly throttled into reverse. The runabout settled into the calm water and stopped.

David grinned. "Good job. See the difference in your control when you slow her down first?"

He'd almost phoned this morning to tell Justin he'd pick him up later than seven, but he'd decided against it. He was glad he had because the kid had been waiting on the porch when David drove up. At this point, he couldn't afford to do anything to risk the tentative link he hoped was forming between them. He needed to tread a fine line between bonding and laying down the law. "After school Monday, you can start stacking the firewood like I showed you."

Justin nodded. "What about Harper?"

"I want to question Rick Kellogg and Pete Delaney when I go on duty today. Then I'll talk to Harper."

Justin tensed. "Do you always have to be a cop?"

Only with every fiber he owned. Being a cop gave purpose to his life. He liked the challenge, the action and the sense he was doing his part to protect innocent people from violent predators.

But after Corry's death, he'd wanted to do more to head off teenage crime and drug abuse, so he'd put his counseling degree back to work. That way he didn't make arrests only to have the kids back on the streets and in trouble quicker than he could turn around. What he tried to do was show the less-hardened ones how to straighten out their lives and become productive members of society. "That's what I am, Justin. A cop."

"Well, Rick and Pete are my friends." He scowled like a little bulldog protecting his territory.

"Your friends need to get caught before they decide they can get away with bigger and bolder crimes. How much older than you are they?"

"Two years. They're in Melody's class."

"Why do you hang out with older guys?"

Justin narrowed his eyes suspiciously. "What do you mean?"

"Don't you like some of the boys your own age?"

"The kids in my class are nerds. But Rick is cool. He knows all kinds of guy stuff."

"What kind of guy stuff?"

"Like how to be tough and not let people boss you around. Mom and Melody are always trying to tell me what to do, but I'm a guy. Guys think different than girls."

"Yes, they do. But girls have a lot of good ideas. Don't automatically discount what they have to say, Justin."

"They don't know much about boys."

"Moms know a lot more than you think. That's what I figured out when I got older."

Justin stared out at the water. "All the guys at school listen to Rick."

"Why? Because he's a good guy or because the boys are afraid of him?"

Justin glowered at David. "*I'm* not afraid of him. He knows a lot more than the other kids. About…you know… The boys ask him questions, and if Rick doesn't know, he asks his brother. Or his dad. His dad is a doctor."

Ah, a doctor. Justin was talking about birds-and-bees questions. He *was* getting to that age. So one of the things Justin got from Rick was access to a surrogate father. A dangerous connection considering Rick's penchant for vandalism. A connection that had to be broken. How to do that and maintain that fine balance between bonding and laying down the law was the challenge. "If you want, you can talk to me."

Justin frowned, his chin jutting. "Why would I wanta talk to you?"

"I don't know. Maybe because I'll listen. Or maybe because we used to be pals."

"Well, we're not pals anymore."

"Why not?"

Justin narrowed his eyes. "For one thing, you're a cop. I can't even tell Rick and Pete about the *Solo*, or they'll know I talked to you."

"You have a point. You'll have to keep our time together to yourself for now."

"If you go after Rick and Pete, they'll think I snitched." The kid looked ready to swim to shore.

"If they bragged about breaking Harper's windows at school, you aren't the only one who can give me their names. I'll question some of the other kids before I talk to Rick and Pete. That way they won't know how I found out about them."

Justin cocked his head to one side. "It might work."

It better work. With a little luck, maybe David had made it through that quagmire. A large cruiser sped by. David reached over to steer the boat into the wake. "How old is Rick's brother?"

Justin stared fixedly at swells of water racing toward them, and the *Solo* bounced with the jolts when they hit. "I don't know. Old enough to drive. He got his license last month, and his dad gave him a brand-new, red Saab for a birthday present. You should see it."

Oh, boy. All Justin needed was to be racing around

while a fledgling driver showed off his powerful new car. "Has he given you a ride in his new Saab?"

Justin shook his head.

David squelched a relieved sigh. But the longing on Justin's face said he would eagerly accept an invitation when or if Rick's brother offered one. And if Rick was a shining example of the Kellogg family, David had a really bad feeling about his older brother. "What's Rick's brother's name?"

Justin squinted. "Why?"

David shrugged. "Just curious."

"Maybe he doesn't have a name." Justin bit his lower lip and turned to stare at the water, effectively shutting David out.

David clenched his jaw and held on to his patience. Building trust with wounded kids took time, he reminded himself. But time was a commodity he was running out of for today. He had to run Justin home and get some serious sleep before meeting his partner at the firing range.

Anyway, weekend boaters and sailors dotted the lake by now, and Justin's nose and shoulders glowed pink from sunburn in spite of the sunscreen he'd slathered on his fair skin. David glanced at the sun. "It's almost eleven. Let's head in."

Fierce concentration on his face, Justin eased the shift lever forward. The idling boat increased speed and glided toward shore.

David smiled at the boy's intensity. This kid had a lot of try. No problems in intelligence or diligence, either. As they sped toward the shoreline, David pointed out his pier.

Justin made a slight adjustment in direction and steered directly for the dock with the Green Bay Packers windsock shifting in the mild breeze.

"Cut the throttle and approach at a thirty-degree angle."

Justin pulled back the throttle, then frowned. "Where is the thirty-degree angle?"

Leaning toward the boy, David grasped the steering wheel with one hand and guided the bow close to the pier. "Now shift into neutral."

Justin obeyed, and the boat slowed almost to a stop.

David turned the wheel. "Now reverse, then cut the engine." The boat stopped and the stern swung toward the dock. Standing, he pointed to the back starboard side. "Grab the stern line for me." He hopped out onto the pier and knelt to secure the *Solo's* bow.

The rope in one hand, Justin tried to climb out of the boat, but the stern drifted too far from the pier for his short legs to reach. He stood frowning at the gap of water that lay between him and the dock.

Chuckling to himself, David reached out and dragged the runabout back to the pier. Gripping the side of the boat, he took the rope from Justin and waited for him to scramble out. "Don't worry. You'll grow."

"When?" Justin asked disgustedly. "I'm the shortest kid in my class. I'm probably gonna be little like my mom."

A vision of Nan popped into David's mind. Her

vivid blue eyes. Her kind smile. The memory of her softness and warmth in her backyard last evening fired his blood. Still on his knees, he wound the rope around the cleat on the dock and floundered to regain his composure. "Your dad was close to my height, so I think you'll grow quite a lot. Just give it time."

"Do you think I'll be big like my dad?" Justin's voice hitched in a breathless little betrayal of emotion.

David's heart clenched. "Yeah, I do." Dragging his eyes to the boy's face, he met his intense gray gaze. "You miss him, don't you?"

Justin's chin jutted as though he wanted to fight the world.

Poor kid. How could a little boy understand why his father had been taken away from him? David didn't understand it. Not with his own father or with Corry. He wanted to slam his fist into something. Instead, he made a conscious effort to let go of the anger.

He climbed to his feet and waited for Justin to determine the direction of the conversation. David had learned not to jump in. Kids often didn't want to talk about a lot of things adults assumed they did.

Justin bent, picked up a pebble and flung it into the lake. "How come you never came around after Dad died?"

The kid sure didn't stick with easy questions. "I should have."

Justin squinted at him, sizing him up with the wisdom reserved only for children. "How come he got shot and you didn't?"

Sharp pain pierced David's heart. He closed his eyes

and drew in a heavy breath. He'd asked himself that question more times than he could count. Opening his eyes, he narrowed them on his dead partner's son. "Nobody ever told you what happened that night?"

Justin glowered sullenly. "You never came around. Who else was I gonna ask?"

"Yeah, good question." David clenched his jaw, struggling to subdue the sickening guilt threatening to choke him. *Just stick to the facts. You owe the kid.* "We got a tip that night that a bunch of kids were shooting drugs in a deserted alley. Your dad was senior officer, so he led the way."

Justin's eyes narrowed as if to defend himself against the words.

David paused, not sure he should go on. Not wanting to go on.

"What happened then?"

"You sure you want to know?"

"I want to know."

"One of the kids fired a gun the second he saw us. I disabled him. But it was too late for your dad." He shoved his shaking hands into his pockets.

Justin lowered his gaze to the dock and kicked at the rough boards with the rubber toe of his shoe.

Life had been so damn unfair to this kid. David swallowed his anger and waited for Justin to say something.

Finally, the boy raised his head and squinted. "How come you didn't see the kid had a gun?"

Another question he'd never been able to answer to his own satisfaction. "It was dark in the alley."

"You should have protected my dad. Isn't that what partners are supposed to do? Protect each other?"

David cleared his throat. "I'm sorry I let your dad down, Justin."

"It doesn't matter if you're sorry. Sorry doesn't change anything. I want to go home."

"Sure." David felt as if he'd been kicked in the gut. Obviously, Justin didn't have Nan's generous spirit. He blamed him. For Corry's death. For living instead of Corry.

How in hell was he going to overcome all that blame so he could help the kid? Especially when he knew damned well he deserved it.

David stood, his trusty .38 in his outstretched hand ready to fire again. He scanned the projected image on the distant wall of the firing range, carefully choosing his targets. He began firing. *Bam. Bam. Bam. Bam. Bam. Bam.* "Ninety-eight percent accurate," the computerized voice droned in his earphones.

Not perfect, but good enough for now. He holstered his weapon, removed the earphones and made a wind-up gesture to his partner who stood a few feet away.

Mike nodded and took aim.

David ducked quickly through the soundproof door into the hall. He ambled over to the soda vending machine, inserted coins and collected a couple cans of Pepsi. He'd promised Cindy he'd talk to Mike about all the extra shifts Mike had been taking on. David hated getting involved in friends' lives, but the social worker was so unhappy, he'd found himself agreeing to her request. He shook his head. What in the hell good could he do? He didn't know one thing about married life. But he'd promised, and he guessed he'd put off the talk long enough.

Mike strode up.

David handed him a can of Pepsi. "Want to get a bite to eat before we go on duty?"

Mike took the can of soda and snapped the tab. "Sure. I'd invite you home for a sandwich, but Cindy's not feeling well."

"What seems to be the problem?" David took a long drink of soda, then gave Mike a serious scowl.

Mike shifted his weight and stared at the floor. "Damned if I know."

"I suppose you've asked her."

"I think she's had about all she can stomach of my job. She resents the extra hours."

The opening David needed. "Maybe she has a point. I've noticed your name on the board for a lot of extra shifts lately."

"I'd rather work than go home and fight with my wife." Mike clenched his jaw.

Now that David had opened the proverbial can of worms without Mike telling him to butt out, he might as well push the issue. "What do you and Cindy fight about?"

Giving David a frown, Mike tipped back his head and drained the can of soda, then crunched it in his hand and tossed it into the recycling bin.

Obviously Mike wasn't going to share his personal problems. David sure couldn't blame him. At least, he could tell Cindy he'd tried. He drank the last of his soda and tossed the can into the bin. They strode to the Jeep in silence, and David opened the door. "I'll drive. You can pick up your car later."

With a nod, Mike strode to the passenger side and got in.

David started the motor and drove out onto the highway. "Nau-Ti-Gal okay?"

"Sure. To answer your question, we fight about everything."

Oh-oh. It looked as if David wasn't off the hook just yet.

Mike wiped his hand over his face in obvious agitation. "'We'll beat the odds,' she used to say. But she doesn't say it anymore. I'm beginning to think the odds are too stacked against us. I hate fighting."

"Do you fight about your schedule?"

"Mostly. But lately, she's gotten it in her head she wants a baby."

"A baby?" David peered at Mike in surprise. Cindy hadn't mentioned a baby. If she had, he would have told her she was crazy. "What is she thinking?"

"Yeah. What do I know about being a dad? My old man split right after I was born. Besides, I'm a cop, and I don't want to worry about a kid. I told her that going in, and she said it was okay."

"If she agreed to no family before she married you, why do you think she wants a baby now?"

"She says she doesn't want to be left alone if something should happen to me. What kind of reasoning is that? If that happened, God forbid, then she'd have to raise the kid all by herself.''

Like his mother. Like Nan. A very hard road. Although neither woman had ever given the slightest hint they regretted being mothers. No matter how hard things got, his mother had always insisted he was the best part of her life. And Nan seemed to feel that way about her kids too. He turned into the Nau-Ti-Gal parking lot, pulled into a parking space and killed the engine.

Mike made no move to get out of the Jeep. ''Having a baby would be a mistake. And making another mistake won't fix the first one.''

David cringed inwardly. It seemed like Mike was forgetting why he and Cindy had gotten married in the first place. David needed to say something helpful, but what? What could he say that could possibly do any good? ''You still love her, don't you?''

''Maybe love isn't enough.'' Mike unlatched his door, then turned and met David's eyes. ''Maybe I should have been smart and stayed single—like you.''

''Staying single might be smart, but it can feel awfully lonely and empty sometimes.''

David squinted at the hot sun beating through the Sunday early-morning haze and strode up Nan's sidewalk before he could change his mind. After he and Mike had supper last night, they'd spent the next twelve hours chasing the devious and unlawful citizens of Dane County. He desperately needed sleep. How long could a man survive without it?

He could probably have set up Justin's schedule with Nan on the phone. But he was here now. His finger over the doorbell, he paused. Would she be up by seven-thirty on Sunday morning?

"Hi, David," Brenda's chirpy voice greeted from the dimness inside the house.

"Hi. You're up bright and early."

Her scrubbed little face appeared above the wood panel of the screen door. "You wanna watch *CHiPs* with me? Jon and Ponch wear all-tan uniforms, not dark brown shirts like yours. We have to watch them on Mute because Mel and Justin are still sleeping. Jon and Ponch ride motorcycles. Do you ride a motorcycle, too?"

His tired mind groped to keep up with her. "Nope. I ride a dull car."

"What color?"

"Tan. Dull color, too." Right now *dull* best described just about everything. And hot. He couldn't wait to get out of his scratchy uniform.

"I'll draw a picher of your car. Wanna see my picher of your boat?"

"Brenda. Who are you talking to?" Nan's voice asked.

Dullness vanished. Birds sang, sun sparkled, air took on a fragrance he hadn't noticed.

"David's here," Brenda announced.

Nan's golden head appeared behind Brenda. She smiled tentatively, her blue eyes full of surprise, her lips turning up at the corners to reveal those dimples in her cheeks.

How could she look so delectable at seven-thirty in the morning? Golden curls framed her delicate face like a halo. Her sundress exposed her creamy shoulders and arms and neck. Her pulse pounded invitingly at the base of her throat.

"Good morning." The intimate hush of her voice settled between them.

He gazed into her wide eyes until she lowered them to his shoulder. But not before he recognized the flicker of hunger.

A pink flush tinged her creamy throat and wandered to her cheeks.

He had no right to be so damned happy, but he must be beaming. The way he felt, he couldn't do much else. Energy poured through him as if he'd slept for hours, but he still couldn't seem to think. And thinking was crucial.

She unlocked and opened the door to him.

The screen door between them had given him a measure of composure. Anxiety gnawing at him, he stepped into her house and closer to her. She smelled like heaven.

He shifted uncomfortably. He couldn't afford to allow his conscience to relax for a second. That little flicker of interest he'd seen before she'd averted her gaze had him so agitated he didn't know what to do. He launched into his reason for being here. "I stopped by to set up Justin's schedule. I thought maybe two hours after school Monday, Wednesday and Friday…"

Still focusing on his shoulder, she drew in a deep breath, her full breasts rising and falling.

That stopped him. He tried to think. The synapses were definitely short-circuiting in his tired and over-stimulated brain.

"You want to know if Justin's schedule will work?" Her smile held him captive, and her mouth formed seductive shapes and sounds.

He stared at her lips, his throat dry, his palms sweaty.

"Are you just gonna talk?" Brenda stood at Nan's elbow, her little face screwed into a frown.

He'd forgotten Brenda was in the room.

"Yes. David and I need to talk."

With a huff, Brenda turned on her heel and marched back to the television.

"He can ride his bike out to my place after school."

She frowned. "How far will he have to ride his bike?" She kept her eyes focused on his shoulder.

He tried to turn his attention to Justin. "About two miles."

"What about traffic?"

"There's very little traffic and a wide, blacktopped shoulder. They redid the road this spring."

"Is your home awfully isolated? I'm uncomfortable with Justin riding his bike two miles along a country road. So many things could happen to him."

"There are lots of houses and cottages, and several retired people are home during the day."

"I'd really need to see the route he'll take."

"I can show you where I live."

"Now?"

He hesitated. The anticipation of sitting close to her in his Jeep fired his imagination. Not exactly helpful.

She glanced nervously at her watch. "I'd have to wake Melody and Justin first." She seemed flustered.

"Can I go?" Brenda asked eagerly.

Yes, a five-year-old chaperone might be a good idea. He nodded.

"You're still in your jammas, honey. I think you'd better eat breakfast and get dressed or you won't be ready for church."

David swallowed hard. A quick trip to set Nan's mind at ease, then he'd drop her off and head home. Could he handle it? Sure he could, unless his useless mind could come up with a reason for not taking her to his place.

While Nan directed Brenda and roused Justin and Melody, David wandered around the living room studying the family pictures crowding every available surface. Sheba, sprawled on the couch bathing herself, halted in midlick to eye him.

David picked up an enlarged snapshot that included him with Corry and the kids, David's old boat in the background. Nan had taken the picture at the end of a wonderful day. Probably about a week before Corry died. Chills chased through him.

Nan studied him from a few feet away.

He slowly set the picture down on the table. "A happy memory."

She nodded, but she didn't smile. The pain in her eyes clutched his heart.

Longing to comfort her and to draw comfort from her almost overwhelmed him along with a massive wave of guilt. He couldn't hold her; he wanted it too much. He couldn't trust a simple hug to remain simple.

Jamming his hands into his pockets, he strode for the door and led the way to his Wrangler. He opened the passenger door, waited for her to climb in, then slammed the door. "I can put the top up."

"No. Leave it down. My hair is wash-and-wear, so no problem there." She gave him a small smile.

He strode around the back of the Jeep, got in behind the wheel and concentrated fiercely on driving through Northport.

"Justin was guarded about his morning with you yesterday, but I know he's excited underneath. Thank you, David."

"Justin's a great kid."

"He really is."

"He's just mixed up about how men should behave." Around Nan, David seemed a little confused about that himself. "He's very angry with me."

"He always resists help. I'm sorry he's being difficult. But I'm sure he'll thank you someday for all you're doing for him."

"He doesn't need to thank me for anything. He needs to learn not to trust boys like Rick and Pete. He's at the age where he needs to learn how to channel his energy."

Channeling energy could be a daunting task sometimes. He turned the Jeep Wrangler onto the lake road.

"He'll need to cross the lane of traffic at this intersection. We'll have to warn him."

"They've done a nice job on the road with plenty of room for bikes on the shoulder. And I'm glad there are more houses along this stretch than I remember. Why did you move out here?"

"I found this great piece of land I couldn't pass up." It *was* a great piece of land, but moving hadn't occurred to him until Nan and the kids left the city.

"It isn't a coincidence that you moved to Northport. Is it?"

He frowned. Not a coincidence at all. "Somehow, I thought I could protect Corry's family if I lived close by. Not too rational, but it made sense to me at the time."

"Why didn't you let me know?"

He drew in a painful breath, remembering his bewilderment after Corry's death. His anger. His depression. He blew out a stream of air. "Hell, I was no good for anyone. Not even myself.".

She sighed. "I wanted to withdraw from life, too." Her voice was so quiet he had to strain to hear her. "After the funeral, I was numb. Emotionally, I retreated to a sanctuary of unfeeling emptiness. But there was so much to take care of. So many decisions to make. I couldn't hide for long because the kids needed me…which was a good thing. But I missed you, David. We all did."

His heart contracted as if a hand had reached in through his rib cage and squeezed. He'd hurt her by staying away. "I just couldn't face you. Or the kids."

She laid her hand on his arm. "You can't blame yourself for what happened."

Who else could he blame? He clenched his jaw and stared fixedly through the windshield. "I'll never be sure if I didn't see the gun, or if I saw it and hesitated because the perp was a kid."

"It was dark in that alley. And if you did see the gun, Corry must have seen it, too. The shooting wasn't your fault. Any more than it was his."

He mulled over her words, but he couldn't bring himself to agree.

"You're focusing on the wrong thing, David. Instead of focusing on the reason Corry died, try thinking about the reasons you're alive."

He gave her a puzzled frown.

"Look at the work you're doing with teenagers now. You're making a difference in kids' lives. Just like you're trying to make a difference with Justin."

He shook his head. "Justin wouldn't need me if Corry was here. He blames me, too."

She sighed. "I'm hoping we can still find a way to get through to him."

"I hope so, too."

Silence hung between them.

"Tell me about your house." Her tone held a decided determination to change the subject.

Relieved, he cleared his throat and launched into one of his favorite topics. "It's a log house."

"A log house?" she asked a little too brightly.

"I did most of the work myself."

"Really?" She gave him an encouraging smile.

"I lived in a mobile home on the beach and spent every minute I had on it."

"Where did you learn how to build a house?"

"I learned as I went along, mostly from books." He grinned. "Of course, the guys at work had free advice for me, some of it useful and a lot of it worth what I paid for it. I haven't done much with the interior. No walls. I left it open and built a sleeping loft across one end. It works fine." He guided the Wrangler around the curve where the lake spread into view and tiny whitecaps frolicked across the sun-drenched water.

"What a beautiful view." She stared at the landscape intently, the wind tossing her curls around her face like wisps of golden silk.

He wanted to take her for a ride in the *Solo*. He wanted to take her waterskiing again. He wanted to take her in his arms.

Not smart. He pulled into his driveway, killed the engine and shoved open his door. "Here we are."

"Your home is beautiful." She stared up at the two-story log structure.

By the time he got around the Jeep, she'd opened the door. He stood attentively waiting while she scooted forward on the seat and stretched one shapely leg to touch her sandaled foot to the ground. Stepping back to allow some space between them, he tried not to notice the provocative way her breasts moved when she leaned forward to push herself out of the Jeep.

He slammed the door shut, turned and walked rigidly around the side of the house. He dared not touch her elbow to guide her. He couldn't be sure where that might lead.

"I'll bet you live on the deck in the summer."

"As much as I can."

"You have such a spectacular view. Is that the capitol dome across the lake?"

"I told you it was a great piece of property." Shoving his hands into his pockets, he strolled beside her to the water's edge.

"I love the sound of the waves washing up on shore." She walked onto the pier and scanned his runabout.

Gulls called. The breeze whipped her skirt around her legs and riffled her hair. The hot sun sparkled off the water, bathing her in golden highlights. He'd never seen anything more beautiful.

"The *Solo* is a sporty little boat. It looks well equipped for waterskiing," she called.

He joined her on the pier. "She's very safe. She has a modified deep-V hull which gives her more stability, and a jetdrive engine. And no propeller for swimmers to worry about." He sounded like a boat salesman.

"According to Justin, she's a dream to maneuver." The greenish-blue color of her dress subdued the blue of her eyes and revealed mysterious shadows in their fathomless depths he'd never noticed before.

He needed to focus on something else. He couldn't keep looking at her and remember not to touch her. If he touched her, he'd kiss her. Then his conscience would never be clear again. He had to take her home now, drop her off and head back to his place. But he didn't want this time to end. He drew his hands out of his pockets.

She glanced at her watch. "I'd better be getting back."

He nodded. All he had to do was turn around and lead the way to his Jeep.

A gray-and-white flutter overhead, and Joseph the seagull settled near her feet. She watched the bird strut, her expression animated and unguarded. Warmth and curiosity shone from her eyes, her lips curved enticingly and her soft skin radiated an invitation to be touched. She looked up at him, amusement in her eyes. Amusement that died the second she met his gaze. "David?" she whispered.

Everything disappeared but her. He covered the two steps between them.

Holding his gaze, she reached out and laid her hand on his chest.

He took her sweet face in his hands and watched her eyes widen in anticipation. Then he lowered his head and touched his lips to hers.

Chapter Five

David tasted of salt and sun and need. His lips demanded, but his trembling fingers held her face with gentleness and respect. Were it not so, Nan might have twisted away. But as it was, she softened her lips and responded to his kiss with an urgency all her own.

She leaned into his warmth. She shouldn't do this. She didn't want this. She had to go home. Get her kids to church.

He enfolded her in his arms and gently pulled her closer. She went willingly, wrapping her arms around his waist. No simple hug this, she reveled in his hard chest muscles pushing against her breasts, his thighs intimately brushing hers.

He deepened the kiss, his lips hot and smooth and moist.

Her heart rate pounded off the charts. She couldn't catch her breath. Emotions, impulses, sensations made her dizzy. Her nerves came to life, creating a feeling of want.

And everything seemed so good. So right.

He lifted his head, his dark eyes searching her face. Crushing her to him, he pressed his lips to her neck.

She gasped crazily for air.

He held her while she struggled to regain her equilibrium. She'd never experienced anything like this before. She was sure of it. She would remember.

He raised his head. She saw the struggle in his dark eyes, felt the tension in his muscles. Laying his hand on her cheek, he stroked his thumb over her lips. Her mouth quivered at his touch. More than she'd ever wanted anything, she wanted him to kiss her again.

A gull squawked and her senses returned. They were standing on his pier in broad daylight, for heaven's sake. David gazed at her as if he'd never really looked at her before, his eyes dark and deep and filled with desire. Desire she wanted to stoke. Bewildered, she backed away.

"I shouldn't have done that," he said huskily.

She drew in an unsteady breath. "No."

"You are so beautiful in the sunshine with the wind blowing your hair. But I…shouldn't have kissed you."

She licked her lips. She could still taste him. The salt. The sun. And the need. "Beautiful?"

"Oh, yeah." His voice was gruff.

He thought she was beautiful. Imagine that. But the

way he was clenching his jaw told her he wasn't a bit happy about it.

"I need to take you home." He grasped her elbow and guided her silently to his Jeep while her mind reeled to deal with his heat, his scent. His kiss.

One kiss. That's all it was.

No, that's not all it was. The intensity with which she'd returned his kiss not only made her feel guilty, it scared her to death. If she felt so guilty and it scared her so much, then why did she wish he'd kiss her again?

They reached the Jeep. Frowning, he waited while she settled herself into the seat, then he slammed the door and walked around the front of the car. Lean and muscular and potent, a dream of a man. And he'd just kissed her witless. Amazing.

She fingered her wedding ring. What was she doing kissing her husband's best friend? She shivered. What had she been thinking? The way he'd kissed her, the depth of longing he'd communicated—this had been no casual kiss.

She remembered how she'd clung to him, how fervently she'd returned his kiss. She'd responded like a love-starved widow, no denying that. A warm flush of embarrassment crept up her neck.

He climbed in behind the wheel. Glancing over at her, he caught her unguarded alarm. A cloud drifted over his face. Gripping the steering wheel, he started the Jeep and pulled out of his driveway.

What could she say to break the tension, to reassure herself that their kiss hadn't changed things between them when she feared their kiss had changed everything?

For the first time since he'd kissed her, the full ramifications of the situation hit home. Her friendship with David hung in the balance. Their kiss meant he obviously thought of her as more than a friend. And she couldn't deny she'd been eyeing him with more than friendship in mind in spite of her guilt. Their kiss… She swallowed. Their kiss… She closed her eyes to shut out the longing enveloping her.

"We can't be more than friends, David. Even if I wanted more, you're a county deputy, for heaven's sake. And you love the danger and excitement of your job just as Corry did. I worry about you as it is. But getting involved, depending on a deputy again, would be crazy. For me and the kids."

"I know that." He silently concentrated on the road ahead, his stern profile and the tension in his shoulders belying his calm facade. "I'm the guy who believes cops have no business with families, remember?"

"Good. That's good." Trying to calm her battered nerves, she closed her eyes, clasped her hands in her lap and welcomed the hot, humid air whipping her hair and caressing her face. Not knowing what else to say, she settled into uneasy silence and tried to focus her mind on what still had to be done at home before she and the kids could leave for church. But she couldn't keep herself from stealing glances at David, glances that fed the turmoil inside her and scuttled any semblance of order in her mind.

He soon pulled up in front of her house. Before she

could stop him, he jumped out of the car and strode around to open her door. She brushed him as she pushed herself out to stand. An electric current vibrated through her body, shaking her to the tips of her toes. She drew in a startled breath.

He met her eyes.

Her heart beat like a triphammer. "You don't have to walk me to the door."

He raised his hands in front of him in a gesture of surrender. "I'm sorry. I don't know what else to say."

She couldn't deal with this chaos going on inside her. She wanted to feel his arms around her again and his lips on hers. But she *couldn't* want that. She just couldn't want...that.

Well, her maturity had to count for something. If she'd gained any wisdom at all, she knew *wanting* something and *needing* it were entirely different things. She might be attracted to men again. Well, to David, anyway. But she'd just have to get over it, that's all.

David lounged in a deck chair wearing his swim trunks, the hot sun melting some of the tension from his muscles. Licking his lips, he savored the taste of Nan. Her scent still seemed to permeate the very air he breathed. The memory of her soft, yielding body this morning on his pier drove his heart mercilessly. He shouldn't have kissed her. But at that moment he couldn't have done anything else.

And she'd responded to his kiss. Wow, had she ever responded. Longing pounded through his blood.

She hadn't been with a man since Corry died. Of course, a vibrant woman like Nan would be vulnerable when caught off guard by the friend she trusted.

The problem was, that kiss had magnified his hunger for her. Now that he'd tasted her, inspired passion in her, he wanted to possess her.

Out of the question.

Possessing her would take commitment and permanence. Things he knew deep in his gut he couldn't give her. He was a deputy, for crying out loud.

But experience had taught him that trying to run away from his feelings wouldn't work. He'd tried that with his grief and guilt after Corry died. If the captain hadn't insisted David get counseling, he didn't know how he would have dug himself out of the hole he'd been sinking into. The counselor had taught him to "defuse the explosive potential of his obsessive grief" by identifying his feelings and making a conscious decision to deal with them.

And hell, he knew denying his emotions did not help him control his behavior, the obvious case in point being his behavior this morning. He'd never decided to kiss Nan; he just had.

Could he apply the defusion strategy to his attraction for her? If he faced her and acknowledged his feelings, could he put his fascination behind him and move on?

The next evening large drops of rain splattered the windshield as David sat in his Jeep around the corner from Nan's house. She should be returning from her university class soon, and he didn't want to alarm the sitter by waiting in front of the house.

He hoped he knew what he was doing, but he had to deal with his feelings for Nan. Trying to ignore them hadn't gotten him anywhere, that's for sure. Still, would facing his obsession head-on really defuse the explosive potential? In theory, yes. Hadn't it worked when he'd used it with his grief for Corry?

He had to do something. He couldn't go on night and day obsessing over Nan. He had to take charge as he did in every other area of his life. He could do this.

Then why were beads of sweat pouring off his forehead? Maybe because he'd forgotten to open the window. He rolled it down and welcomed the gusts of rain blowing in his face.

Finally, Nan's little blue Toyota pulled into her driveway. He waited a few minutes, then pulled up in front of her house and darted through the downpour to her porch, nearly colliding with the portly, reddish-haired, red-faced woman bustling out the front door. Whoops. He'd forgotten all about the baby-sitter.

Nan stood in the doorway, the porch light bathing her in its soft glow. "David?" She sounded alarmed, probably worried Justin had done something to warrant David's being here.

He gave her what he hoped was a reassuring grin. "Don't worry. Everything's fine."

The worry on her face didn't dissipate. "Kate, this is David Elliott. He's the Dane County deputy who's working with Justin. David, Mrs. Kate McDuff."

Mrs. McDuff eyed him up and down. "Top of the

evening, Officer. I hope you're not here on official business again." The woman thrust her hand toward him.

He shook her warm hand. "No, ma'am."

Kate McDuff aimed her umbrella at the porch ceiling and triggered the mechanism. It shot up and opened like a parachute. "I'm afraid our Justin has a chip on his young shoulder."

David couldn't explain the rush of protectiveness he felt at her criticism of Justin. "He's a healthy boy, Mrs. McDuff. And a good worker. He stacked a sizable pile of wood after school today."

"Well, healthy boys can get in a lot of trouble. I'm awfully glad you'll be taking him under your wing. It puts this little mother's mind at ease, I'm thinking." Mrs. McDuff's head bobbed with each word like one of those little dolls in people's car windows. She began to shuffle past him.

"Nice meeting you." He ducked around the lady's umbrella.

"Same here, Officer."

"Good night, Kate," Nan said.

"Good night, dear." Mrs. McDuff hustled into the night, wrestling with her umbrella in the blasts of rain.

He focused on Nan.

Holding the screen door open, she shifted her gaze away and offered her face to the mist blowing into the shelter of the porch. "Looks like quite a storm moving in."

"Sure does." He could stand here discussing the safe topic of weather, or he could go through the door she held open. Jamming his hands into his pants pockets, he stepped into her cozy living room. He caught a whiff of her scent, light and fresh, and the memory of kissing her silky neck almost swamped him with longing.

She pulled the screen door closed and focused a wary eye on him. ''Justin really did okay tonight, or did you say that for Kate's benefit?''

''Actually, things went better than I'd hoped. After he stacked wood, we had time for some soccer. He's great at it. I think he should play on a team. Team sports are a good way for kids to channel their energy. And being on a team would give him a sense of belonging. He seemed to like the idea when I suggested it.''

A smile brightened her wary eyes. ''That's wonderful. Then he's being more cooperative?''

''When he doesn't think about it too much.''

She sighed.

''Try not to worry. He'll come around.'' And he probably would. Eventually.

She shifted uncomfortably as if waiting for him to leave.

''May I come in for a few minutes?''

''Sure,'' she said stiffly. ''Would you like a soda? Or a bottle of mineral water?''

He cleared his throat. ''Mineral water sounds good.''

She brushed past him.

The house was so quiet. Her kids were in bed. Like in the dreams invading his sleep every night. He fol-

lowed her into the kitchen, the sway of her hips enticing him to new levels of appreciation.

What in the hell was he doing here? This cockeyed
plan of facing his obsession was clearly not working.
Instead of defusing the explosive potential, he had the
unmistakable feeling he'd poured gasoline on a blaz-
ing inferno. Somehow he needed to extinguish the fire
in his blood. Pronto. He had to make sure he didn't
give her reason to be skittish about being alone with
him.

She disappeared behind the refrigerator door covered with crayon drawings. He recognized a red and
orange version of the *Solo,* only because the name was
printed in uneven red letters across the bow.

Nan closed the refrigerator door.

He pointed at a drawing of a brown-clad, misshapen
figure standing beside a brown car. "I think this is
me."

She nodded, a hint of laughter in her eyes. "I hadn't
noticed your shorter leg before." She was obviously
trying to dispel the tension between them.

He could probably try to do his part. "Cute. I don't
see any pictures of you. Do I smell censorship here?"

She handed him a bottle of mineral water. "Do you
want a glass with ice?"

"This is fine." He stifled the impulse to grasp her
hand.

She pointed to one of the drawings. "That's me."
A figure with narrow blue eyes, messy yellow hair and
a mouth turning down stared back at him.

He chuckled. "Were you having a particularly bad day?"

"Apparently. Brenda told me my attitude needed adjusting." Her eyes shone with love and amusement. She looked especially soft and vulnerable when she talked about her kids.

"Let's sit in the living room." She walked away.

He followed her. As much as he tried not to, he couldn't help noticing her hips doing their delightful little dance. Sheets of rain pelted the windows, and thunder rumbled low and ominous.

Settling herself on the couch, she slipped her feet out of her sandals and folded her slender legs beside her.

He took a swig of mineral water, his hand unsteady. Maybe sitting down would be a good idea. Lowering himself into the leather recliner, he allowed his eyes to roam from her explosion of curls to the tips of her bare toes and back again. Longing pounded through him, driving his heartbeat harder, faster.

She tipped her head back and drank from her bottle of sparkling water.

He watched the movement of her silken throat, the hunger to touch her hammering at his good intentions.

She turned a tentative smile on him, the smile not quite reaching her eyes. She looked as nervous as a suspect being read her rights.

Fighting the need to touch her, he clenched his hands around the bottle of water. Touching her would not reassure her. Anything but. If he made a move, she'd probably ask him to leave. Then where would he be? He needed to find a way to ease into this. He squelched the urge to reach over and tip her chin up so he could make eye contact with her. "How long have we known each other?"

She looked at him as if his question baffled her.

"It's been five years. You'd just given birth to Brenda."

"Of course, I remember. You and Corry were transporting a prisoner to Chicago when Brenda was born. When you got back, you came to the hospital with Corry." A hesitant smile flitted across her face. "You were so amazed by Brenda's tiny fingers."

Warmth crowded his heart at the memory. He'd been amazed by both the baby and her beautiful mother. "I'd never seen such a perfect human being." He held her gaze. He might as well say it. "We've been friends for a long time, and nothing needs to change between us unless we want it to."

"I *don't* want it to," she said emphatically.

Disappointment registered. He quashed it. "I don't either." He sounded equally convincing. "But I think we need to be honest with each other."

She pulled her gaze away. "Of course, friends should be honest with each other." She drew in an uneasy breath. "Why did you come over tonight?"

"I wanted to see you." There. He'd admitted it. He gulped the water. "Is that so bad?"

"That depends."

He waited for her to tell him what it depended on. He hated her feeling ill at ease with him, and knowing he had only himself to blame didn't help.

She finally raised her eyes to meet his. "As long as we're being honest, I need to ask you a question."

He gave her a nod. "Fire away."

"The David I remember didn't believe in marriage and wanted no emotional involvement with a woman. Has that changed?"

Now it was his turn to look away. He focused on his bottle of water. "I don't believe in marriage for cops," he corrected.

"Because of your father."

How could he explain the rage of a lonely little boy who missed his father? The helplessness of being too young to help his mother in her struggle to provide food and shelter? The frustration of living with a step-father who provided the material things but gave no love? "Because of what my father's death did to my mother and me."

"But you became a cop, anyway."

"I waited until after my mother died. She couldn't deal with my being a cop like my dad. So I joined the Navy when I graduated from high school."

"What about after the Navy? Weren't you ever tempted to marry anyone?"

"I didn't have the time or the money. After the Navy, I went to college. Then I worked as a high school counselor for a couple years." He realized he was going on and on, probably telling her a lot more than she ever wanted to know. "That's pretty much the story of my life."

"Not quite. Your credentials are excellent if I were

interested in hiring you for a job, but I'm much more interested in your personal life."

He glanced in her direction. "What do you want to know?"

"Why you've never married and had a family when you enjoy children so much. I've watched you with mine."

"I have a lot of fun with your kids." And he should have been there for them after their father died. He drew in a long, slow breath and studied the floor. "The only girl I ever thought about marrying was my high school sweetheart, but we were too young to get married."

"What happened to her?"

"Her family moved to Seattle our senior year. We wrote for a while, but gradually other things filled our lives and our interest faded. We were kids. Later, I wanted to be a cop, which left no room for marriage and family. You already know how I feel on that issue. But I've always dated." What did dating have to do with anything? He wasn't making sense.

She met his gaze as though trying to understand. A tiny frown line appeared between her eyes. "Is that why you kissed me? You want us to date?"

He raked his hand through his hair. "Would you like to go out with me?"

She thought a moment. "I'm afraid dating would jeopardize our friendship." She leaned forward, her eyes imploring as if she expected him to reassure her.

He didn't know how. Hell, she had to realize that kiss had launched them into uncharted waters. And the way he felt right now was anything but safe. Just as it wasn't smart. Or practical.

She looked away, her eyes darting here and there as if she couldn't find a place to rest them. She heaved a deep sigh, her full breasts rising and falling.

The memory of her softness pressing against his chest claimed his attention, desire burning through him with fervor. "It seems to be complicated between us," he admitted.

She nodded in agreement, then she frowned. "The only thing I know for sure is that I'm confused. One minute I feel as married as I ever did. The next minute I—the next minute…" She absently twisted her wedding ring.

Pain wrenched his heart. What was he doing to her? He had no right to rip her out of her safe emotional place. He had nothing to offer her. "I'm sorry."

She looked at him miserably. "Please don't say that. You're not responsible for my confusion. I'm trying to explain that I might be sending vibes that tell you I'm interested in more than friendship. And I don't mean to."

He wanted so desperately to reassure her. What a hell of a mess. "Your vibes are just fine. And you have no reason to feel guilty."

"I feel unfaithful. How can I be committed to Corry and enjoy kissing you?"

He hated this. His own guilt was one thing. He deserved guilt. "You're a young, vibrant woman. Your husband's been dead for two years, for crying out loud."

"You mean I'm a love-starved widow."

Damn. He was really botching this. He shook his head slowly while his mind scrambled to figure out a way to dispel her guilt. "That's not what I mean. You're a beautiful, intelligent, warm woman. That's why I kissed you. Not because you're a widow and not because you're sending out vibes, but because of the special woman you are."

Tears glistening in her deep blue eyes, she peered at him as if trying to determine whether or not he was telling her the truth.

And he hoped with all his heart she believed him. If she didn't, he didn't know how to convince her except to hold her and kiss her again. And then he'd be lost. He was sure of it.

She swiped at her eyes and gave him a tentative smile. "You're awfully good for my ego, you know."

"I hope so. I think your ego could use a little boost." He returned her smile. He couldn't help feeling as if he'd avoided a land mine.

She drew in a deep breath, the frown line appearing between her eyes again. "Do you think we could just enjoy being together sometimes?"

His heart swelled with hope. Fixing his gaze on the floor, he fought for reason. He knew damn well this was not the best idea.

"I've been so lonely, and it's been wonderful being with you again." She pressed her fingers to her temples as if trying hard to sort out her thoughts. "Neither of us wants anything complicated."

He tried to beat back the hope that had his heart

pounding. "Do you think we could keep it uncompli-
cated?"

"I don't see why not." Her words rode a little puff
of air. "Can we try?"

Try? Try what? A simple flirtation? An affair? Or
was she asking if she could depend on him to keep
his feelings in check? No more touching? No more
kisses? "What kind of relationship are we talking
about?"

"You know, just enjoy being together? Have fun?
Maybe you could come to supper sometimes like you
used to. And we could do things with the kids once
in a while?" He heard the loneliness in her voice.

Loneliness she wanted him to fill. God, how he
wanted to spend time with her. "I like being with you.
But I'm not sure what kind of relationship we're talking about."

"Just friends, David. I'm not ready for more than
that. And we already talked about the deputy thing."

"So no dating? Or kissing?"

She frowned and shook her head.

Could he be satisfied with keeping things light and
fun? With not touching her? Not kissing her? What if
he couldn't pull it off?

Who was he kidding? She filled the aching emptiness inside him. The emptiness that had been part of
him so long he'd almost accepted it as normal. He'd
do whatever it took to pull this off. He gave her a
fleeting grin. "We could both use some fun in our
lives."

Chapter Six

"Cool." Eyeing the Saab's shiny dashboard, Justin ran his hand over the smooth, red leather of the front passenger seat. He'd never been in such an awesome car before.

Settled in the driver's seat, Rick gave a twist on the steering wheel as if he was really driving the Saab instead of it being parked in his garage. "Ben's not home now, but maybe I can convince him to give you a ride someday. I gotta tell you, he was very impressed with you, Kramer, for not giving the cop my name that night in the alley."

"I would never snitch on you, Rick."

"I guess I had you all wrong. So, is your mom gonna make you pay Harper for the smashed windows?"

"Yeah."

"Where are you going to get the money?"

No way could Justin tell Rick about the job David had given him. He dragged in a heavy breath and decided to lie. "I don't know."

Rick reached across the seat and punched Justin's shoulder. "You want some good news?"

"Sure." Justin could use some good news.

"Ben said to ask you if you want to work for him like me and Pete do."

"What kind of work do you do?"

Rick narrowed his eyes. "What kind do you think?"

Justin stared at Rick and tried to figure out what he was getting at. "Like the night at the drugstore? You and Pete were working for Ben then?"

"Duh. Jeez, Kramer, sometimes I wonder what planet you've been living on all your life. Harper keeps cash in his back room in a metal box. And Ben says the old man doesn't lock the drugs away, either. You'd think Harper would wise up after all the broken windows. But I guess he thinks kids go around smashing windows for fun or something." Rick hit his forehead as if he couldn't believe Harper's stupidity.

Justin tried to smile, but his face muscles felt stiff. Rick and Pete had lied to him. They'd said they were hungry that night.

"The problem is, Harper lives above the drugstore, and his bedroom must be near the front. The old buzzard can still hear too well. That's why we ended up trying that little window in the alley. And if that stupid cop hadn't gotten lucky…''

Justin swallowed hard and looked out the wind-shield at the rakes and tools hanging on the inside wall of Rick's garage. If David hadn't shown up, Justin would have helped in a robbery. Jeez. Dad would never have understood Justin's getting involved in a real robbery. That was serious stuff.

''So what do you say?'' Rick eyed Justin.

Justin didn't want to hear any more about Ben's job, but he couldn't let Rick think he was a wuss, either. ''I don't know, Rick. The police know us now, you know.''

''What difference does that make? We'll never get caught again. If you would have been smart enough to jump, you woulda gotten away too.''

''You guys left me hanging from that high window, remember?''

''It wasn't so high.''

Justin swallowed into an aching throat. ''The cops aren't stupid, Rick. Now that they know about us, they don't have to catch us. If anything is missing, they'll come straight to us.''

''In Northport maybe. But we won't be stuck in this burg now that Ben has wheels. He says the pickings are too slim here, anyway. We've been staking out some lake houses closer to Madison.''

Justin didn't want to know all this stuff. He felt sick, kind of like he might throw up. He focused on Rick again.

Rick grinned. ''It's a perfect setup, Kramer. You

need money. And we need a little guy like you to fit in tight places we're too big to get through.'' Rick narrowed his eyes. "Unless you're chicken."

Justin dragged in a shaky breath and tried to bluff. "Give me a break. I don't want cops breathing down my neck, that's all. I'll give the job some thought."

"Well, don't think too long. Ben will give you a good cut. And he's not going to be happy you have to think about it. I don't have to tell you to keep your lips zipped about this, do I?"

"No." Justin shook his head solemnly. "You don't have to tell me."

A surge of elation took Nan's breath away as she emerged from Marshall Field's after work. David stood with his broad back to her, studying the mannequins in a display window and trying to look inconspicuous in his brown and tan deputy uniform. She wondered if he was aware of the smiles he was eliciting from women shoppers as they ogled him.

He turned and spotted her, a grin igniting and spreading.

She floated to him like a hummingbird to a rose.

"I bought you something." Jostling his duffle bag, he handed her a box of Marshall Field's special chocolates.

The ones she'd die for. "I love these things."

"I must be psychic. Or maybe I was blessed with a good memory."

She smiled her appreciation and focused on unwrapping the chocolates. "Want one?" She popped a morsel into her mouth, its rich taste instantly rewarding her effort.

He shook his head and watched her chew with fascination.

A flush warmed her.

Finally he focused on her eyes and winked mischievously.

She laughed. It was either that or swoon, and she didn't want to make a total spectacle of herself in the middle of the mall.

"I just got off duty. Didn't take time to change clothes, or I would have missed you. It's a beautiful day out there to play."

She drew in a deep breath of regret. "I'd love to play, but you're forgetting I have three children waiting for me at home."

He cocked a brow and peered down his nose at her. "I've checked the parenting manual, and nowhere does it say you are not allowed a little time to recharge your batteries before you head home to your kids. Do you think Mrs. McDuff will mind staying an extra hour?"

In spite of herself, she considered his suggestion. She couldn't remember when she'd last taken a break before going home to her family, unless it was to grocery shop which probably didn't count. She had so many things to do at home, she really shouldn't consider it. She looked into his expectant eyes and realized how much she'd like to be with him. Just for a little while. "I'll call Kate and see."

He grinned his lopsided grin, grasped her elbow and

began steering her down the wide corridor. "While you call her, I'll duck in the rest room and change clothes."

Doing her best to ignore the shimmer of heat zinging from his hand on her arm, she concentrated on taking coins from her wallet.

"Those shoes could be a problem." He frowned at her high-heeled pumps.

"What are you planning?"

"You'll see. I can always carry you."

An inviting thought but probably not a practical one. "I have walking shoes in my car."

"Great." He stopped beside her at the pay phone. "Got enough change for your call?"

"Right here." She plucked the receiver off the hook and slipped coins into the slots.

Without another word, he disappeared into the men's room.

Kate answered on the third ring and assured Nan she had no objection to staying an extra hour and would stay longer if Nan needed her.

David emerged from the men's room in khakis and a green polo shirt that set off his dark features like nobody's business. Without meaning to, Nan ran her eyes over him, appreciating him until she felt light-headed and flustered. Heat crept up her neck. "You look smashing," she muttered.

He chuckled and gave her a wicked wink. "Thank you. Did Mrs. McDuff agree?"

Nan nodded. "She's a jewel. I'm very lucky to have her."

"Terrific. Let's get those shoes, shall we?"

After retrieving her walking shoes from her car, they settled into David's Jeep and sped out of the parking lot like a couple of truant teens. Butterflies of excitement frolicked in her stomach.

David guided the Jeep into traffic. "Set your stop watch. The hour begins now, and I aim to impress on you that I'm a punctual man."

"Where are we going?"

Glancing over at her, he gave her an amused frown. "Next, you'll be asking if we're there yet."

She chuckled. "I'm not used to being abducted or taken anywhere I haven't planned myself."

"That's the point. Relax, enjoy those chocolates, and we'll be there before you know it. I want you to meet a few of my friends."

She'd thought they would spend the hour alone, and she couldn't help feeling a little disappointed even if she was curious about who he wanted her to meet. But she did as she was told. Settling back in the seat, she unwrapped another sinfully rich candy, tossed it into her mouth and studied the passing landscape to determine exactly where they were headed.

When he pulled into a parking space at the Vilas Park Zoo, she couldn't have been more surprised. He jumped from the Wrangler, jogged around the front and opened her door for her. She climbed out and waited for him to move out of her way.

But he stood tall and immovable, looking down at her with eyes dark and intense.

She stopped breathing and knew only his heat, his

scent, his strength. Every cell in her body rejoiced at his closeness.

"You smell like heaven," he murmured. "Heaven and chocolate."

Her lips began to tingle. Too bad they'd agreed on no kissing.

Dragging in a deep breath, he clasped her hand and pulled her into a lope beside him.

Her feet responded of their own volition because she was too dazed to motivate them. He pulled her faster and faster. She tugged her restrictive skirt higher to accommodate her strides and ran like the wind. The air swished through her hair like freedom itself, and her spirit took wing. By the time he slowed in front of the tiger enclosure, she was breathless and giddy.

"Meet Clarence and Oscar and Moriah." With the seriousness of introducing royalty, he pointed each cat out in turn. "The others must be taking a nap." His breathing held no hint of his run.

Why she should be surprised, she didn't know. He was a man of action and obviously in terrific shape. Her own lungs, on the other hand, were clamoring for oxygen. Her lack of fitness was downright embarrassing.

David kindly didn't seem to notice. "Listen up, big guys and gal. This is Nan Kramer. I expect you to treat her with the respect and dignity she deserves. Even if she does run like a girl."

She laughed, which only used up much-needed oxygen. There was nothing to do but to bend forward, her hands on her knees, and drag in air until her lungs were satisfied.

"She needs to learn how to play," he explained to the cats who eyed him with lazy reserve. "And I've taken it upon myself to teach her."

She raised an eyebrow. "Oh-oh. Why does that declaration strike fear in my heart?"

"It shouldn't. I'm a gentle teacher."

"I'll wait and see."

He grasped her hand. "No more running. We'll amble from here."

He was a man of his word. Hand in hand, they ambled to the pens enclosing the camels and giraffes. "That's Bernie." David pointed to a camel with one of his humps tipped precariously to one side. "Bernie has a little trouble with balance, but Helen, the statuesque and perfectly endowed camel in the corner over there, dotes on him. I think being lopsided is an aphrodisiac for camels." He dropped his voice as though sharing a secret.

Nan wrinkled her nose in disbelief.

As if on cue, Helen lumbered over to nuzzle Bernie's chin.

David lifted a knowing brow. "See? Do I know my camels?"

"And I'm *very* impressed with your knowledge. Just how much time do you spend here?"

"As much as I can. Can't have too many friends, you know."

She frowned. She hardly ever took time to be with

friends, even the human variety. Of course, when would she find the time?

David walked on to the giraffes, moving leisurely, fluidly, with understated power. She followed. Three beautiful animals peered down their lofty, graceful necks. "Delilah, Krenshaw and Mopsy." He pointed each one out.

The tallest giraffe turned and glided away.

"Krenshaw is an aloof aristocrat, but Delilah and Mopsy are just folks."

Nan laughed. "I can see that."

David grinned. "You have a great laugh. I'd like to hear it more often."

"I laugh a lot," she said defensively.

"Not around me."

She shot him a mischievous smile. "You're usually not this funny."

He arced a brow and tried to look offended, although the grin curving his lips spoiled the effect. "I'll have to work on that." He ambled on.

She strolled beside him, chuckling at his introductions to shy emus, haughty ostriches and sturdy zebras. Circling wide, he guided her past the bison and the lineup of black bears and grizzly bears and polar bears. Finally they stopped in front of the sea lions' enclosure.

Several sea lions slid into the water. They splashed and frolicked as if they'd rehearsed a show for anyone who stopped by to watch them. "There's Fred and Al and Clancy and Richard."

"Which is which?"

"Take your pick. Can you tell them apart?" He stood looking down at her, a pensive smile on his lips.

She shook her head.

"Neither can I. They have subtle differences, but I can never remember who is who." He grinned and peered conspicuously at his watch. "The bewitching hour is almost here, I'm afraid. I must get you back to your subjects."

"So soon?" She couldn't keep the disappointment out of her voice. An hour had never flown by so fast.

"We'll come back again, I promise." He turned and began strolling toward the parking lot.

She fell in beside him, trying to control the impulse to grasp his hand and pull him to another animal display. She didn't want to forsake her lightheartedness just yet. The swings in the playground nearby beckoned invitingly. She couldn't resist. Feeling like a carefree child, she jogged over and sat in one.

Chuckling, David walked up behind her and gave her a push.

She cruised through the air, hardly believing how reluctant she was to return to the real world. The world where she was a responsible mother of three children who were expecting her at home. The world where one never knew when or where danger lurked for a sheriff's deputy.

Denying the minutes ticking by, higher and higher she flew, noting the sun bouncing off the water in Lake Wingra as she floated on the wind. Breathless, she anticipated David's touch when she returned to the ground. The touch that sent her flying high again.

*   *   *

Nan walked out of the University of Wisconsin's Bascom Hall to find a soft drizzle of rain clouding her vision of the twinkle of lights up State Street and the glow of the lighted capitol dome in the distance. The night held the surreal quality of *Brigadoon.*

Like a dream, David stepped out of the mist near the Lincoln statue and strode over to her, a giant black umbrella hovering above his head.

She was definitely glad to see him, but she still hadn't adjusted to the buzz of excitement his nearness evoked. Of course, he was so darn attractive, she wouldn't be normal if he didn't have an effect on her. She needed to relax and enjoy the effect, that's all.

He wore jeans and a deep-blue Henley shirt that stretched valiantly across his broad chest and made her fingers itch to touch him. "Hi." He gave her his lopsided grin, the one that made her knees go weak.

She smiled. "Hi. Don't you know enough to stay out of the rain?"

He stepped close and held the umbrella to protect her too. "I thought maybe you'd forgotten your umbrella."

He was taking care of her, and she couldn't be more touched. She drew in a deep breath. "How'd you know?"

"Maybe I *am* psychic. Or maybe I knew because it wasn't raining about the time you had to go to class." He raised a dark brow. "Hungry? Or thirsty?"

She shook her head and concentrated on keeping herself from melting into a little puddle at his feet.

"Want to walk in the rain?"

"I'd like that." What they did wasn't important. Just being with him for a little while was all she needed before she went home to her sleeping children.

Silently she walked beside him, sharing the intimacy of his umbrella. He smelled of fresh air and sunshine and David. A giddy little giggle bubbled inside her. Feeling more alive than she had in a very long time, they strolled up State Street. She noticed displays in shop windows, smelled scents wafting from various eateries, heard the chatter of passersby and snatches of music drifting on the warm, damp air. Everything seemed vital and new, yet old and familiar at the same time.

A guitar player strummed an Eric Clapton ballad near the old Brathaus. Without warning, David slipped his arm around her waist and swirled her in a circle with him. "Just dancin' in the rain," he intoned.

She laughed with surprise. And with happiness. When she stumbled against him, he laughed and steadied her.

They walked on in shared silence, her state of well-being increasing with each step. She couldn't remember feeling so right with the world. So feminine and protected and cared for. She had the most irresistible urge to slip her arm around David's waist and snuggle into his warmth, but she didn't give in to it.

"Remember the night you and Corry danced on State Street for the department relay to raise money for the Food Pantry?"

Smiling, she nodded. "We should have had an umbrella that night."

"Most couples ran for cover when it started to pour."

"Corry was never one to run for cover."

"No, he wasn't. But neither are you. You always held your own with him. I remember thinking what a good sport you were that night."

"Thank you. Even if I did end up looking like a drowned rat?"

He chuckled. "You could never look like a rat, drowned or otherwise."

"Hmm. You're too kind."

"He'd be glad we're friends again, don't you think?"

She looked up at him, a soft glow warming her heart. "Yes, I'm sure he would."

"We used to have great times, didn't we?"

"Mmm."

"I miss those times. The ones with the kids, too."

She smiled. "Yes."

"Let's take them waterskiing some Saturday when I'm off."

She nodded. "Only if you'd like to. Don't let Melody wheedle you into it."

He chuckled. "They're great kids. I've missed them."

She reached out and squeezed his hand. "We've all missed you. We Kramers may not be as interesting as your zoo friends, but we have our good points. Hey, I can cook."

He gave her an amused look. "You sure can. And

you smell better, too. But you enjoyed my zoo friends, didn't you?''

"I did. Though I'm a tad anxious about competing for your time," she teased.

He raised his brow. "Give me a nice, safe tiger anyday?"

"Something like that."

"Words to live by. But I don't think tigers like walking in the rain."

"A shame."

They climbed a shallow flight of stairs to the deserted capitol building. David folded his umbrella, and she realized the rain had stopped and a few stars twinkled in the sky. She pointed. "There's the North Star. We get to make a wish."

"Why?"

"What do you mean, why? Haven't you heard the rhyme? 'Star light, Star bright, first star I see tonight. I wish I may, I wish I might, have this wish I wish tonight.'"

He shook his head, his lips curving at the corners. "I lived in New York City, remember? I never saw stars until I moved to the Midwest. By then, I was too old for rhymes."

She looked at him askance, unable to determine whether he was teasing her or speaking the truth. "You're never too old for rhymes. Come on, make a wish." She closed her eyes and thought about what to wish for. She wished for Justin to find his way and for her family to be safe. And...she smiled inwardly. She wished to have fun with David. But she was already doing that. She could wish to be in his arms—no, she couldn't wish that. She opened her eyes. "Did you make a wish?"

"I don't need to." His words were hushed.

"Why not?"

"Listen." He grinned.

The faint strains of Elvis's "Can't Help Falling in Love with You" drifted from a radio hidden by the night.

David laid his umbrella on the low wall lining the sidewalk. Without another word, he stepped close. Locking her with his intense gaze, he grasped her hand, took her in his arms and began moving slowly to the music.

She clasped his shoulder, the soft fabric of his shirt smooth under her fingers, his muscles hard and unyielding under her hand. Following his lead, she smiled into his dark eyes and drifted in the still night. Wrapped in his heat, the pressure of his hand on her back and the brush of his body as they moved to the music coaxed her to lay her head on his chest.

But she couldn't give in to the temptation. She and David had agreed to have fun together. Nothing more.

Her wish to be in his arms had come true in spite of her trying to thwart it. The only problem was, she liked being here even more than she'd anticipated. All she needed to do was to relax and enjoy the dance. If she could just slow down the breathless exhilaration racing through her, making her as dizzy as a schoolgirl with her first crush.

The song on the radio ended, and an announcer's

voice droned indistinctly. David didn't seem to notice. He kept right on guiding her around the sidewalk to a rhythm that had nothing to do with the one on the radio.

She blissfully followed, dreading the end of the dance when they'd have to separate.

Chapter Seven

Nan fussed with her unruly curls, dabbed on a little makeup and slipped into her white sundress, telling herself she would do the same for any dinner engagement. Her flustered nervousness and the color in her cheeks told her she was lying to herself. She touched perfume to several pulse points and walked out of her bedroom.

"You look very pretty, Mom." Melody beamed as if Nan's dinner with David was her idea.

Brenda sniffed. "You smell good, too."

Justin had been sulking in his room most of the day and didn't peep his head out now. She was worried about him. Something was bothering him, but he wouldn't tell her what it was. She'd mentioned it to David when he'd called to invite her for dinner. Maybe he could get Justin to open up.

A sharp knock on the front door announced David's arrival. Brenda bounded to the door and let him in.

He'd dressed up, too. He wore a blue silk shirt with gray slacks and was even more drop-dead gorgeous than ever. She did her best to censor her reaction for her children.

He stared across the room at her, not even dragging his eyes away as he acknowledged Brenda's chatter.

Nan's nervous tension shot up a few degrees.

"You two enjoy your evening and don't worry about a thing," Kate clucked. "Come on, girls, let's go in the kitchen and have some ice cream." She bustled out of the room, but the girls stayed put. Unfortunately, David held more appeal for them than the ice cream did.

"Where are you going for your date?" Melody asked.

Nan cringed. "Melody…" She'd explained she and David were having a just-friends dinner.

"We're going to a new Italian place near Waunakee." Though his words were for Melody, his eyes didn't wander from Nan.

She glanced nervously from Melody to Brenda. They both beamed at David, total approval in their eyes.

"Where's Justin?" David asked.

"He's been in his room all day." She could hear the worry in her voice.

"Shall I try to talk to him before we leave?"

"Would you?"

"Sure."

"Thank you." Turning on her heel, she led the way down the hall to Justin's room. Struggling to ignore her breathless awareness of David walking behind her, she knocked on her son's door. When he didn't answer, she opened it.

He frowned up from the book in his hands.

"David's here, and he wants to talk to you."

Justin narrowed his eyes. "What if I don't want to talk to him?"

"This isn't negotiable," she said as calmly as she could. She turned to David.

Jaw set, he touched her arm, then moved past her into Justin's room. "I'll be out in a few minutes."

With a sinking feeling, she closed the door and walked to the living room. All she could do was hope for the best. David had gotten through to Justin before. Maybe he could do it again.

Thankfully, Melody and Brenda were in the kitchen with Kate. Nan waved as she breezed past. "Bye, guys. I'm going to wait for David on the front porch." She settled into the porch swing and tried to calm her worried jitters.

But she didn't have to wait long before David strode out, a puzzled look on his face.

"What happened?" She stood up to meet him.

"Nothing. He's not talking to me, either."

Her hopes plummeted. "Oh."

"Give him a little time. He's not a kid who enjoys keeping things to himself. He'll get tired of thinking about whatever's bothering him and eventually want to talk about it. Let's give him some room."

She shot him a worried look.

He met her gaze. "We've done all we can for now."

She tried to smile. The least she could do was make an effort to tuck her worries about Justin away for the evening and try to enjoy dinner with David.

He clasped her elbow, guided her down the steps to his freshly washed Jeep and opened the door for her. He laid his hand lightly on her back to guide her into the car.

She almost winced with the sparks that ignited inside her. While he walked around the front of the car, she tried to calm the sensory overload pounding through her. This was just two friends going out for dinner, for heaven's sake.

He got in behind the wheel and turned to look at her. "You look terrific." Although he rolled the *r*s like Tony the Tiger, she heard the rush of his breath beneath his words.

She gave him a nervous smile. "Thank you. So do you."

"Thank you." He started the car and zoomed down the street. "Hungry?"

She nodded. But food was far from her thoughts. She was too busy dealing with the butterflies making her feel like a high school junior on prom night.

Twenty minutes later, they were seated across from each other at a small table covered with a red-checkered tablecloth and nestled in a secluded corner of the crowded little restaurant. The succulent aroma of garlic and rich Italian sauces made her stomach even more unsettled. The glow from the stubby candle on their table flickered intimately over David's face, highlighting his dark, smoldering eyes.

Her nerves thrummed like war drums signaling attack. She tried her best to quiet her excited anticipation.

"How are your classes going?" His words were innocent enough, but the low tone of his voice only increased her nervousness.

"Okay, I think. Even if I do sometimes feel like a den mother. My quiz instructors are all younger than I am, and most of my classmates are even younger."

He grinned, his even white teeth flashing. "Have you found other students who are going back to school like you are?"

She nodded. "Actually, there are quite a few. And we do our best to give each other support."

"It can't be very easy."

"Finding time to study is a challenge. But my biggest hurdle was convincing myself I wasn't silly. That I belonged there."

"You do belong there. I admire you for doing what you're doing."

He admired her. She met his gaze and sighed. Not a discreet little sigh, but a helpless gulp.

"Are you all right?" He frowned with concern.

"I'm fine."

The waitress appeared to take their drink order.

"You still like Chardonnay?" David asked.

She nodded.

"A Chardonnay and a Pilsner should do it."

The waitress returned with the drinks in record time and left again.

David took a sip from his glass of beer. "Maybe the wine will relax you."

She looked at him in alarm. Relaxed might not be the best idea. She might let down her guard and do something to fan the flames of the fire smoldering inside her.

He drew in a deep breath. "Are you still worrying about Justin?"

"I'm trying not to."

"You seem awfully nervous."

"I'm fine," she lied, and began to study the menu. She could feel his eyes on her as she concentrated fiercely.

"I'd like to make a toast." He lifted his glass of beer. "To old friends."

She met his eyes and saw understanding. He was trying to reassure her. She reached for her wineglass and raised it. "To old friends," she murmured, and took a sip.

"Oh-oh. Don't look now, but some old friends from the department are headed our way." He didn't look any too happy about his revelation.

She fought to keep from turning to see who he'd spotted. "Who?"

"The Gardners and the Chandlers," he said through barely moving lips.

She groaned inwardly. Susan Gardner had always been a relentless matchmaker. Terrific. Just what she and David needed.

"Well, look at you two. What are you toasting? Or is the toast a private one?" Susan raised a curious eyebrow.

Avoiding Susan's question, David stood up and reached to shake hands with the men. "What brings all of you out of the city?"

"This restaurant was reviewed in the *Cap Times*. The food is supposed to be worth the trip." Paul rested his hand on Nan's shoulder. "It's been way too long. How are the kids?" He smiled into her eyes with genuine warmth.

"The kids are great. And it's wonderful seeing all of you again." She smiled and they returned her smile, compassion evident in their eyes.

"Maybe we'll see more of you now. I'm sure David has invited you and the kids to our annual Labor Day department party." Susan peered directly at Nan as though she would not be denied an answer.

Susan assumed they were a couple. But of course she would. She hadn't gained a reputation for matchmaking falsely. Nan swallowed and glanced at David.

"We haven't gotten around to talking about the party yet." David shot Susan a warning look.

"I think we should leave these two alone and get our table. Good seeing you again, Nan." Paul strode away.

Raising their hands in silent farewell, Ken and Amy followed Paul.

"I'll see you at the party, Nan. We'll catch up on news then." Susan squeezed Nan's hand and joined her group.

David sat down and drew his napkin across his knees.

"Susan is still trying to marry you off, isn't she?" Nan tried to inject humor into her voice, but fell a little short.

He gave her a crooked grin. "She thinks everybody should be married. And she's a very stubborn woman."

Nan nodded in agreement. "You're a challenge to her."

The waitress interrupted, took their orders and left them alone again.

Nan sipped her wine.

"Would you like to go to Paul and Susan's party?" David took a drink of his beer.

What would it be like to go to a department party again? "After Corry died, I turned down invitations until people stopped inviting us. I couldn't face the memories. Or the kids and me going alone."

"You wouldn't be alone. You'd be with me."

She drew in a long, pensive breath. "I'd like to see everybody, but I'm not sure how well I'd cope."

He reached across the table and clasped her hand, his skin hot and rough. "I'll help you cope."

She drank in his gentle caring. His warmth. His concern. And she believed him. He'd stand beside her, and he would help her deal with her memories. But going to the party with David might be a problem. "If we go together, people will think we're a couple."

He took a thoughtful swallow of beer. "Everybody isn't as obsessed with pairing people up as Susan is."

Maybe he was right. She gazed into his velvet eyes and recognized the longing she saw there because it mirrored her own. How would it feel to be at Susan's party with him? Was she brave enough to find out?

Nan stood in Susan Gardner's roomy, country kitchen, Melody at her elbow. The last time they'd been here was before Corry died.

"How long have you and David been seeing each other?" Susan innocently transferred hors d'oeuvres to a tray from the cookie sheet she'd taken from her oven, the spicy scent filling the kitchen.

Warmth flushing her cheeks, Nan glanced at Melody as the buzz from the eight or ten women in the room stopped, all ears tuned in to hear Nan's reply. Nervously she reached for words to lay everyone's curiosity to rest. "We're not seeing each other. David has been counseling Justin. He asked the kids and me to your party only because you mentioned it."

An hors d'oeuvre in midair, Susan peered at Nan skeptically. "Oh, come on. You and David were having a romantic dinner together, and Justin was nowhere in sight. I'm very curious about that private toast you were making when we walked in."

Nan frowned, uncomfortable that Melody was taking the conversation in. "I hate to disappoint you, Susan. But we were toasting to old friends. Which is what David and I are."

"Paul said that's the line he's been feeding the guys at work, too, but it isn't the way he's acting." Susan scooped up another hors d'oeuvre.

Nan swallowed a gulp of surprise and stared at her. How *was* he acting?

Her pause wasn't wasted on Susan, matchmaker extraordinaire. "He's acting moonstruck."

Nan drew in a little breath of pleasure, in spite of herself. Then she noted Melody's enthusiastic smile. Great. Melody didn't need more romantic notions about her and David.

"Are you sure he knows you two are just friends?" Susan plopped the last savory morsel on the serving tray.

Nan tried to laugh. "Of course he does. You're such a romantic."

Susan met her eyes. "That's why I know romance when I see it," she said softly.

Nan swallowed a flush of frustration. Obviously, Susan wasn't about to give it up. And Melody had heard too much already. "Would you like Melody and me to take these trays to the buffet table?"

Susan's green eyes twinkled with mischief, a knowing little smile turning the corners of her mouth. "Sure. Getting a little too hot for you in the kitchen?"

Ignoring her, Nan picked up a tray and motioned for Melody to get the other one.

The other women began to chatter as though they hadn't been listening at all.

Nan and Melody made their way to the dining room, returning friends' greetings as they went. They set the trays of hot hors d'oeuvres on the table alongside several other appetizing-looking concoctions. Nan scanned the room for David and the younger kids.

When they'd arrived at the party, Paul had snagged David to lend a hand at the grill in the backyard. And the Gardner kids had commandeered Justin and Brenda to play games in their new downstairs recreation room. Melody opted to stay with her mother. Not a great idea given Susan's matchmaking bent. How could Melody do anything but think she and David were more involved than they were? Nan glanced around the room for familiar faces.

A tall, blond, Nordic-type man stopped piling a variety of goodies on a small plate and peered down at her as if he had trouble focusing. "Have we met?"

She glanced at the amber drink in his hand. "I don't think so. I'm Nan Kramer. And this is my daughter, Melody."

"Hi, Melody."

Melody smiled shyly. "Hi."

He brandished his drink in the air as if making a toast. "Just celebrating my freedom, I guess. I left my wife last night."

"I'm sorry," Nan murmured.

He took a significant sip of his drink. "Being a deputy is damn hard on a marriage. Don't let anybody tell you otherwise."

"Yes, it is," Nan agreed.

"By the way, I'm Mike Manning, Dave's partner. Where is he anyway?"

"Nice to meet you, Mike. David is helping Paul in the backyard."

"That's where I'm headed. Nice meeting you. You, too, Melody." He strode away.

"Nan, it's so good to see you."

She turned toward the pleasant female voice.

Diane Kelley stood beside her, a pretty, pink maternity dress flowing over her round tummy. "Hi, Melody. Nan, we missed you at the last PTO meeting."

"I was sorry to miss it, but Melody had a sleepover, and I wanted to be there."

Diane nodded understandingly. "Are you baby-sitting yet, Melody?"

"I'm taking the course at school, and Mom says I have to finish it before I can baby-sit."

"When you're ready, let me know, okay?"

Melody smiled. "Okay."

Diane turned back to Nan. "Has anybody tapped you to work in the school fund-raising tent at the Autumn Festival?"

Nan shook her head. "Not yet. I'm planning to bake pies, but I'd be happy to help in the tent, too. Just let me know when you need me."

"Do you think David might want to help too?"

Nan tensed. "I have no idea. You'll have to ask him."

"Oh. I assumed you'd know."

"Diane, David and I are just friends."

Diane met Nan's eyes. "Sorry. I'd heard—"

"Here you go, my little wife." Wrapping an arm around Diane's shoulders, Patrick Kelley handed his wife a glass of clear liquid with a lime slice floating in it. His red shirt almost matched his hair and made his round face appear even more cherubic than ever.

"Good to see you, Nan. And this must be Melody, all grown up?"

Melody shifted shyly. "Hi, Mr. Kelley."

David strode into the living room. His gaze swept the room in earnest. Meeting Nan's eyes across the room, he held her gaze, his face melting into his lopsided grin.

Her heart began thudding with delight. Try as she might, she could do nothing to stop the smile curving her lips, igniting and spreading through her until it encompassed her entire being. She felt as if she was glowing like a Christmas tree for Melody and the entire room full of people to see. But she seemed unable to do a thing about it.

He moved to her side like a bee to nectar and searched her eyes. "I didn't mean to be gone so long. Fine support I turned out to be. You okay?"

She nodded, his concern giving her immeasurable pleasure in spite of her awareness that Melody's inquisitive eyes were noting their closeness, noting the way they smiled at each other.

"A little rusty on your manners, aren't you, Dave? You didn't even get your date a drink."

She pursed her lips and waited for David to correct Patrick's assumption that she was his date. And knowing it wouldn't make a bit of difference if he did.

He didn't. "I was too busy cooking food to feed the likes of you, Kelley. Would you like a drink, Nan?"

"No, thank you." She glanced at Melody's beaming face and groaned inwardly.

"Nan agreed to help in the school fund-raising tent at the festival. Can we count on you, too, David?" Diane asked.

He cocked a brow at Nan. "I hope you're not going to let them throw balls at you until you fall into a tank of water."

She shook her head and laughed. "Nothing that exciting. I'll be selling pie and ice cream."

He grinned down at her. "I think I can handle that."

"Great," Diane cooed. "See, Nan? That wasn't so hard."

A questioning frown clouded David's expression as if he wondered if he'd agreed to something Nan didn't want him to.

But she'd love selling pie à la mode with him. She gave him a reassuring smile. "It will be fun."

"I can't wait to water-ski Saturday," Melody blurted.

All eyes focused on her exuberant face.

Nan might have known Melody could be silent for only so long.

"Do you ski often?" Diane asked indulgently.

Melody shook her head. "Not often. But David is taking us out in his new boat. And after we water-ski, we're going to have a family picnic at his house."

Diane glanced at Nan. "Sounds like fun."

The next thing she knew, Diane and Susan would be enlisting Melody's help in their matchmaking schemes. Undoubtedly, Melody would be only too happy to oblige. Nan coughed nervously.

David met her eyes for a moment, then focused on

Patrick. "What about those Milwaukee Brewers? Do you think they can pull themselves out of their slump in time to save the season?"

The men launched into a heated discussion on the merits of their favorite baseball players with Diane adding a comment here and there. Thanks to David, they were no longer the focus of attention, and baseball not being one of Nan's interests, she half listened.

Melody watched David, eyes dancing.

Nan sighed. She could just imagine the thoughts racing through her daughter's mind.

Melody turned to Nan. "This is just like it used to be with Dad," she whispered.

Nan shook her head. "It's not the same at all, Melody. David and I are just friends."

"Mo-om." Melody gave her a look of pure exasperation. "I'm not a little kid. I'm thirteen, for heaven's sake."

Nan stared at her daughter, unable to come up with a single word to discourage Melody's conviction that she and David were a couple.

But even if she could, how could she expect Melody to believe her when convincing herself was becoming so hard?

At the door of the Gardners' house, David waited as Nan gave Susan a parting hug.

Then Susan stretched to hug him. "You're not doing something right, lover boy. Nan's telling everyone you two are just friends." Her words were low and meant only for his ears.

Withdrawing from her, he gave her an indulgent squint. ''You need more excitement in your life, Susan.''

She had the audacity to guffaw.

He strode out onto the porch to join Nan. He'd seen the kids make a beeline down the block to where he'd parked the Jeep. Nan stood in the light of the porch lamp, her blond curls glowing like spun silk around her face, her eyes smiling at him. Her cornflower-blue dress was the same color as her eyes, and it skimmed her graceful body, nipping and flaring to accent her full breasts, her slim waist, her round hips. He swallowed into a dry throat.

Her beauty went much deeper than her appearance. She radiated love and good will to everyone around her. Her beauty was soul deep.

Grasping her elbow, he guided her down the steps, reveling in her closeness, her warmth. ''Did you enjoy the party?''

''Mostly.'' She sounded worried.

He clasped her hand in his, and they headed down the block toward the Jeep. ''What's wrong?''

''Everybody believes we're a couple.''

''Does it matter what they think?''

''I guess not. But their comments convinced Melody.''

''Explain we're not.''

''I tried. She didn't believe me.

''Why not?''

''It's not that simple, David. She misses her dad,

and she likes you. So she wants to believe you're going to be part of her life.''

''I can be. You can tell her I'll be her friend, too. She's a smart kid. She'll understand.''

''She's thirteen, David. And she has a definite romantic streak.''

''You sure are a worrier where your kids are concerned, Nan Kramer.''

She sighed. ''It goes with being a parent.'' She gave him a little smile. ''Did you have fun at the party?''

''I had a great time.'' He laced his fingers through hers, her bones so delicate in his big mitt. ''I loved bringing you and the kids. You all fit right in as if you'd never been gone. It was obvious everybody's missed you. And nobody knew you were worried about coping with your memories of Corry. I was damn proud of you.''

''Were you?''

He gave her hand a squeeze. ''Damn proud.''

''That's the nicest thing you've ever said to me.''

Her words made his chest ache. ''I have lots of nice things I want to tell you. Whenever you're ready to hear them.''

She hesitated.

He pulled her to a stop, cupped her chin and peered into her lovely face, looking for...what, he didn't know. Vulnerability? He saw it. Need? It was there, too. He drew in her fresh scent and fought to remember why he shouldn't take her in his arms and crush her close.

''David?'' she whispered, laying her hand on his chest. A warning? An invitation?

His heart pounded hard, blood roared in his ears, and reasons for fighting so hard to deny his need to kiss her faded into oblivion.

''The kids are waiting in the Jeep.'' Her words sliced through the haze in his mind.

The kids. He closed his eyes for a moment, every nerve and muscle screaming with frustration. He withdrew his fingers from her chin, but he still clutched her hand, unwilling to break the connection. He couldn't step away from her warmth, couldn't tear his gaze from her luminous eyes. He stood there, waiting for good sense to overtake his desire.

He should be grateful the kids were waiting. If they weren't, he'd have given in to his need to kiss her. And from the look in her eyes, she wouldn't have stopped him.

Chapter Eight

Saturday morning, Nan awoke from a wonderful dream and squinted into Brenda's gray eyes. The five-year-old supported her head on her elbows on the bed, nose-to-nose with Nan, the scent of corn flakes and orange juice on her warm breath.

"It's morning, Mommy. The clock's little hand is pointing to six and the long one is on ten, and I'm all ready to go to David's house to water-ski." She pushed herself off the bed to display her pink polka-dot swimsuit.

"It's too early." Nan squinted into the sunlight streaming through the filmy lace curtain. She wanted to go back to sleep and finish her dream. In it, she'd been on a sandy beach with David. Warm tropical breezes blew and palm trees swayed and they sipped piña coladas between kisses.

As long as her fantasies played themselves out in her dreams and not when she was with him, she'd be okay. She wondered if he had dreamed about her since she'd last seen him the night of the party. The night they would have kissed if she hadn't remembered the kids waiting in his car. She'd been so disappointed. Even when she knew kissing was not what she and David should be thinking about or doing.

"Mommy. Justin and Melody said we'll be too late. We ate breakfast and everything."

Nan yawned sleepily. "David isn't expecting us until ten o'clock. That's four hours, Brenda. Tell Justin and Melody to cool it."

Brenda screwed up her face.

Nan pointed to the door. "I'm awake."

Sighing noisily, the little girl trudged from the room.

Nan punched her pillow and tried to doze. Too late. The dream had vanished. But today her real life included David. She smiled, anticipation and excitement stirring her blood.

Sitting up in bed, she stared at her wedding ring. She'd never wanted to be with any man but Corry. He'd lived next door growing up, and she'd idolized him from her inferior four-years-younger status until she finally grew up. She'd been nineteen and on spring break from her freshman year at the university when he came home to visit his parents. He'd finally noticed her. And they'd married less than two years later.

But of course, this was different. She wasn't falling in love with David. She wouldn't let herself fall in love with another cop. Maybe she'd been able to live with the fear of loving one once, but that was before her fears had been confirmed. Before the father of her children had been gunned down by a fourteen-year-old so high on drugs he didn't know what he was doing.

She shoved away remembered grief.

She was building a life for herself and her family. Except for Justin's problems, life was predictable, well ordered and safe. Just what her children needed after the trauma of Corry's death. Just what she needed, even if she did find things a little dull occasionally.

That's why she loved having David in her life. He was fun, and he brought an element of excitement to her predictable life. He made her feel young and attractive. And alive. She sighed. And, yes, he made her feel like a woman.

David edged the *Solo* alongside the dock and cut the engine. He had her fueled and ready for her special passengers this morning. And what a morning. Sun blazed through the early September haze, a soft breeze blew and the temperature had already climbed into the eighties. The promise of a glorious day lay ahead.

He couldn't wait to see Nan. He'd worked and swum himself into exhaustion since the night of the party, and she'd still filled his thoughts and dreams until his desire to be with her had become an aching need. All week he'd found himself grinning for no reason and whistling snatches of melodies. Today, he was going to have fun with her and her kids. And he was as excited as a kid himself.

He climbed out of the runabout and secured her hull, a flutter of gray and white settling on the pier beside him. David peered at the gull eyeing him expectantly. "Sorry Joseph, nothing for you today."

Tires crunching gravel announced his guests' arrival. He had all he could do to finish securing the *Solo*'s stern before he took off in a jog with a bounce in his step and a tune on his lips.

Justin charged across the lawn toward him, the boy's normal sullenness taking a back seat to his excitement. A good sign. "Hi, Justin."

"I'm gonna be goalie." The kid beamed with pride.

David grinned. "Great job."

"Coach said I looked like I knew what I was doing."

"Didn't I tell you? You're a natural athlete. Just like your dad."

Justin pursed his lips and gave a proud little nod. "Our first game is next week if you wanta come watch."

David's grin broadened. "I wouldn't miss it. How about today? Are you psyched for waterskiing?"

"Yup." The boy headed fulltilt for the beach.

"Justin," Nan's soft voice called. "Come and get the cooler." She stood near the deck, her little body lost in the large yellow shirt hanging to her knees.

David had all he could do to breathe. He struggled to gain some semblance of composure while his legs automatically carried him to her side. He couldn't stop grinning like an idiot. Towering over her, he tried to stuff his hands into nonexistent pockets in his swim trunks.

"Good morning," she said quietly, touching his arm as she smiled into his eyes.

He covered her small hand with his and fought to keep from folding her into his arms.

She withdrew her hand and spread her arms to encompass the world. "Did you ever see a more beautiful day?

"Never." The day matched the woman, he wanted to say, but he stopped himself. It was one of those things she probably wasn't ready to hear. He stood and beamed down at her lovely, joyful face and tried not to feel too arrogant because maybe, just maybe, he had something to do with her lighthearted attitude. "The *Solo* is all ready to go."

"I need to put some things in your fridge first."

"Hi, David," Melody and Brenda greeted in unison. They both were decked out in swimsuits, sunglasses and beach shoes. Cute as hell, like their mother.

"Good morning," he answered.

Melody probably looked the way Nan had as a teenager. She had Nan's shining blue eyes as well as that zany explosion of curls.

"This day will be so much fun." Melody almost danced with excitement. "It's a family day like we used to do."

David smiled at her enthusiasm and motioned to the

enormous black bag she grasped in both hands. "What do you have there?"

"Our family wish bag." She glanced at her mother and laughed. "Mom puts everything in here we could wish for. Snacks and sunscreen and dry clothes and stuff. It's supposed to go on the boat."

"Herman and Lizbet are in there, too," Brenda piped up.

"Her water wings." Melody rolled her eyes.

Brenda bobbed her head up and down in confirmation.

He grinned and ruffled the little girl's hair. "Melody, you can set the bag on the pier, and we'll load it when we're ready to go."

"Okay. Do you want to put anything in the family wish bag, David?" Melody asked.

"Thanks, but I travel pretty light."

"Okay." Melody jogged toward the water.

"This goes in the boat?" Justin sauntered by, gripping the handle of a red cooler.

David looked at Nan. "The cooler goes, too?"

"It's filled with mandatory soft drinks. We *don't* travel lightly."

"Guess not. You can set the cooler on the dock, Justin."

The boy dutifully strode toward the lake.

"Are you sure you're ready for us?" Nan arched a teasing brow.

David grinned into her vivid blue eyes. "I couldn't be any readier. I've missed you."

"Me too you." An intimate hush in her voice, she smiled up at him.

He ached to hold her, to taste her throat and the creamy skin just above the blue swimming suit he glimpsed inside her unbuttoned shirt.

She turned and headed around the side of the house. "Our picnic is in the car."

Blowing out a stream of air, he followed her.

Brenda fell in beside him. "Is your house made out of giant Lincoln Logs?"

He focused on her question. Lincoln Logs? He'd spent countless hours building with those things when he was a kid. He studied his house for a minute. "Kind of, I guess."

"Can you see the logs inside, too?"

He nodded. "Want to see?"

Her eyes widened. "Can Mommy see, too?"

"Sure. Let's help her carry the food inside."

"Do you like Popsicles? They're my favorite. I like red the best. What color do you like?"

Popsicles. How many years had it been since he'd eaten one? His mother used to make them out of fruit juice when he was little.

"Don't you know what color you like?" Brenda eyed him expectantly.

He tried to remember his favorite Popsicle flavor. "Grape. Uh, purple."

The little girl pursed her lips in consternation. "Oh dear. I don't think we brought purple."

Realizing what a serious problem this was, he

clamped his lips together to keep from smiling. "Don't worry. Red sounds great."

Her little forehead puckered in a frown. "If we didn't bring enough red, you can have half of mine."

"Thank you. You're very generous, Brenda." Like Nan.

Nan stopped near the raised hatchback of her Toyota and turned, a smile lighting her face. "I hope you realize Brenda doesn't share her red Popsicles with just anyone."

"I like David, Mommy. Maybe he can be my new daddy."

A lump lodged in David's throat. He swallowed hard. "I'm honored, Brenda."

Nan looked stricken. "Brenda, little girls can't just pick out a daddy."

"How come? Jennifer gots a new daddy."

Nan knelt at the little girl's level and peered soberly into her eyes. "Jennifer's mommy got married. That's why she has a new daddy."

Brenda's gray eyes were like saucers. "David's a man. You could marry him and we could live in his Lincoln Log house. It would be fun."

"It might be fun, but it's never going to happen, sweetie."

"Why not?"

Nan shot David a helpless look.

He swallowed again and reviewed his options. Diversion sounded like a good tactic about now. "We'd better get that car unpacked and get out on the lake before it rains."

Brenda focused on him. "Let's hurry, Mommy."

Shooting him a silent thank you, Nan rose grimly and began retrieving items from the hatchback until the ground was littered with them.

He hated that she worried so much about the kids, but he didn't know what he could do to stop her. Except to see that she had some fun to balance out the worry.

Watching her made his day, but maybe he should give her a hand. He took the grocery bags from her, shifted them into one arm and stooped to grasp the cooler handle. "You have enough food to feed a station house full of hungry deputies."

"The kids are always ravenous after swimming." She handed a box of potato chips to Brenda and slammed the hatchback shut. Tucking a thermos in the crook of her arm, she grasped the picnic basket. "Lead the way, sir."

He led the way around the side of the house to the deck where he set the cooler down and held the screen door open for Nan and Brenda to file in before him.

"Look Mommy. Giant Lincoln Logs." Brenda hugged the potato chip box and tipped her head back to take in the two-story interior.

"It's magnificent, David." Nan plunked the basket and thermos on the island counter.

"High praise, indeed." He grinned, pride puffing him up a little. Setting the cooler down, he tried to see his house through her eyes. Kind of a tall box with a sleeping loft across one end of the second story and massive supporting timbers for decor. Probably pretty rustic for a woman's taste. "I guess you'd say I'm totally into form following function."

"It's powerful and solid and inspiring. Like you."

Placing the grocery bags on the island counter, he glanced at her to make sure she wasn't kidding. Nobody had ever called him inspiring before.

She stood in his kitchen looking up at the giant rafters, awe bathing her lovely face. His house seemed so much brighter with her in it.

"Look, Mommy. Such a big fireplace, I could stand in it. I won't, though. David, can I climb the Lincoln Log steps?"

"Sure. Go ahead."

Brenda handed the box of chips to him and bounded to the steps.

"Thank you for saving me out there." Nan's eyes were too serious.

He grinned. "Good thing she didn't check the sky. There's not a rain cloud in sight."

She smiled. "You're so good with her."

"Only trying to impress her mother."

Her dimples winked at him. "I have to put some of the food in the refrigerator and freezer."

"Wouldn't want those Popsicles to melt." He pulled the freezer door open.

It took less doing than he'd anticipated to get the group and their paraphernalia positioned in the *Solo*. Then he manned the throttle while Nan expertly and patiently instructed the older kids' skiing attempts from the stern. Both Justin and Melody proudly made it up on the second try.

Finally David convinced Nan to ski herself.

The *Solo* glided over the water, hot wind buffeting his face. He squinted into the mirror above the steering wheel watching Nan's third try to make it up onto the skis. She was having a hard time, but he knew she wouldn't give up until she made it. And she'd get it soon. Rising shakily out of the water, she stayed in a crouched position, struggling to get her sea legs.

He glanced back at the kids hovering in the boat's stern. Brenda sat in Melody's lap, sucking her thumb. Melody hugged her close in spite of their life vests.

"Come on, Mom," Justin yelled over the roar of the motor. "You can do it." He knelt on the floor gripping the side of the boat with both hands.

Finally, Nan straightened sure and strong and skimmed over the water with skill. Hair whipping, her lithe little body bending and flexing with the jolts of water, she soared free and unafraid.

David clenched his jaw. She had a lot of spunk.

"She did it!" Melody laughed and clapped her hands.

"Way to go, Mom!" Justin hit something with a loud thud.

No sound from Brenda. David glanced back. The little girl frowned on the side bench with her thumb in her mouth. Apparently, Brenda wouldn't be happy until her mother got back in the boat.

Nan's confidence returning fast now, she cut aggressively across both wakes. She beamed with sheer exhilaration. She'd hit her stride and was enjoying the ride.

He couldn't be happier.

"Did you see that, David?" Melody hollered.

"She's doing great." He gave a thumbs-up gesture.

Nan cut across the wakes again at nearly a right angle to the boat.

Beautiful form. Just watching her gave him a thrill. The animation on her face spoke of unlimited energy, but skiing called for strenuous use of muscles that don't often get much of a workout. And she'd been in the water for quite a while now. He raised one hand, the signal to stop.

She gave him the signal to turn. Apparently, she planned to ski back to the dock. He trusted her judgment, but she hadn't skied for a long time, and he didn't want her to overdo it.

He made the turn and glanced in the mirror.

She banked the skis expertly for the turn, then skied straight. Great. No more fancy stuff for her tired muscles.

Watching her in the mirror, he drove the *Solo* toward his pier, exhilaration firing his blood. This day was turning out better than he'd even hoped. Nearer shore, he watched Nan transfer her weight to one leg and gradually lift the other ski off the water, forcing her toes up.

He smiled. She was giving the skier's salute before she quit.

The tip of the ski dipped into the water. The back swung up under the pressure and struck her, its force pitching her forward. His heart lurched into his throat as she disappeared in a spray of flying water.

Briskly turning the boat in a half circle, adrenaline pumped through him like a raging storm. She'd taken a bad fall and the ski had hit her hard. Had it hit her head or neck or shoulder? He didn't know. She could be injured or unconscious. His heart pounded so hard he had difficulty breathing. He had to get to her. Now.

Woodenly raising one arm to warn other boaters of a skier in the water, he raced to pick her up, peering intently at the spot where she'd gone down.

"Do something, David." Melody screeched in a tight, high-pitched voice he'd never heard before.

"Mommy's drowning!" Brenda hurled toward him, shrieking at the top of her lungs. Latching onto his arm, she clung to him like a scared kitten.

"She's not drowning, peanut," he comforted. "Your mom is a good swimmer and she's wearing a life vest, so calm down and watch for her," he yelled to the older kids. Thank God, his voice sounded almost calm.

Holding Brenda in one arm, he steered with the other hand and kept his eyes focused on the water.

"There she is," Justin yelled urgently.

David sucked in a sharp breath. Squinting, he willed his eyes to spot any sign of injury. She was taking so long to move. Or did it just seem too long? His pulse thundered in his ears. He willed her to signal she was okay. She had to be okay.

Finally, she clasped her hands over her head in the signal that all was well.

Relief flooded him in a rush of chills. He hugged Brenda's tense little body and breathed a silent prayer of thanks. Nan seemed to be all right. But he wasn't so sure about her kids. Her kids were terrified.

And why wouldn't they be? Their mother was all they had in this big scary world.

He'd known what it was like to depend totally on his mother. He'd worried about her every time she was a few minutes later than she'd promised. He would have freaked out if anything like this had happened to her.

As far as Nan's kids were concerned, everything she did impacted them. And he had encouraged her to ski. He wouldn't blame the kids if they never trusted him again.

The *Solo* neared her, and he turned off the engine. "Justin, get the boarding ladder over the side."

The runabout coasted closer until Nan handed the skis to Justin and reached for the ladder, her somewhat sheepish smile reassuring. David grasped Brenda's little hand and moved to the stern. He handed Brenda over to Melody and leaned to help Nan climb aboard. The adrenaline ebbing from him left trembling in its wake. He fought the impulse to fold her into his arms. "Are you okay?" he asked quietly.

She met his eyes and nodded. "I'm fine."

The kids pushed between them, Brenda and Melody dissolving into tears and Justin sniffing suspiciously.

Nan hugged them to her, the water still pouring off her delicate body. "Hey, guys, I'm fine. I pushed too hard. I shouldn't have skied so long. I didn't mean to frighten everybody."

"Let her sit down." David grabbed a towel and

handed it to her, doing a quick once-over to determine any visible bruises. That ski had hit her too hard for there to be no bruises.

"My legs are a bit rubbery," she admitted.

"You're going to feel muscles you never knew were there."

"I remember." She blotted her face and hair, then wrapped the towel around her shoulders and settled herself on the bench, the kids clustering around her.

David had to make sure she was okay. "You must have swallowed a lot of water. Where did the ski hit you?"

She peered over Brenda's head while the little girl sucked her thumb and cuddled in Nan's lap. "It hit my shoulder. I think it stunned me."

"Let me see." Alarmed, he dropped to one knee beside her.

Adjusting Brenda in her lap, she stretched forward to allow him a view of her right shoulder.

He drew the towel aside. He wanted to kiss her neck, but the angry red line on her back cooled his ardor. Frowning, he ran his finger along the mark on her smooth skin. No swelling. Yet.

She flinched.

"Sorry. You're going to have a serious bruise. I don't feel any swelling, but that's probably because of the cold water. Melody, get the first-aid kit from the storage unit between the front seats. There's a cold pack in there."

Melody shuffled forward to get the first-aid kit. Justin and Brenda eyed him accusingly.

He drew in a deep breath and averted his eyes. These kids had been through too much, poor scared little things. Their pain and fear made his heart ache. It was clear that losing one parent had set them up to fear losing the other one.

A fleeting thought of life without Nan clouded his mind. Clenching his jaw, he beat the idea back into his subconscious.

He'd plunged in way over his head, no doubt about it. Now he fully understood why Nan worried about the kids getting the idea they could depend on him always being there. Like they'd depended on Corry.

Chapter Nine

The dull throb in Nan's shoulder and neck nagged at her while she hustled around David's kitchen putting food away after their picnic on the deck. David had been tense when they'd come in off the lake. Her fall must have upset him more than she'd realized.

He'd even seemed tense while he coached Justin in some new soccer moves. She knew Justin missed the roughnecking he and Corry used to share. And his growing confidence in David was heartwarming to see. She sure hoped Justin wasn't getting the same ideas about David that the girls were, though. She bit her lip. She needed to figure out what to say to dispel those ideas.

She'd loved watching David play soccer. The sun had collaborated with the sheen of perspiration on his body to spotlight the powerful muscles in his back and shoulders and arms. And his legs. Well, he had the most muscular legs she'd ever seen. Probably from all that swimming and waterskiing. She would love to watch him ski again, but her limited skill in driving the boat didn't allow that. Maybe he'd give her lessons on operating the *Solo*.

"The last of the burgers." David set a plate of hamburgers on the counter. He still wore his black swim trunks, his bronze skin proclaiming many hours outdoors. He looked as if he'd stepped off one of those male pinup calendars. Except for the tension claiming his muscles and furrowing his brow.

Could he be that worried about her fall? She picked up the plate of leftover hamburgers. "I'll put these in the fridge for you to warm up in the microwave."

"I'm not here enough to eat them."

"Where do you eat meals?"

"Usually fast-food places."

She screwed up her face in distaste. "Don't you listen to the news? Fast food has too much fat." She gave him a lingering appraisal. His skin stretched tightly over his rib cage, his stomach muscles were hard and rippled. She sighed in admiration. "Although, I don't think you have much to worry about."

He didn't smile at her comment. Instead, he set his jaw and strode around the island counter to stand beside her, his dark eyes very serious. "We need to talk about the kids."

"What about them?"

He shifted his gaze to peer out the window over the sink. "Damn."

She turned and followed his gaze through the window that looked out on the side yard. Justin stood near the woodpile, talking intently with a bulky boy with a shaved head who swaggered as if he owned the place. She frowned. "Who's Justin talking to?"

"Rick Kellogg."

"*The* Rick Kellogg? What's he doing here?"

"I don't know. Justin wasn't going to tell him that he knew me. I've done some checking with Juvenile Crime. Rick's a kid with problems, not the least being an older brother who's probably going to lead him straight to hell."

She stared at him in alarm. "What do you mean?"

"Rick's older brother, Ben, is a known drug user whose father has bailed him out of trouble with police more than once. Over this past summer, several businesses and homes in Northport have reported break-ins and thefts. Ben is probably behind them, and he's probably using Rick and Pete to help support his drug habit."

A chill shook her. Justin couldn't be involved with anything like that, he just couldn't be. "What is Justin doing with a boy like that?"

"It looks as if they're disagreeing about something. Neither of them looks very happy."

She threw the dish towel on the counter, the pain shooting through her shoulder making her flinch. "I'm going to put a stop to this right now."

David laid his hand on her arm. "Let Justin handle it."

She met his calm gaze, ready to disagree.

"He'll be humiliated if you charge out there. He's not three years old anymore," David said quietly. "It's time to begin trusting him to fight his own battles."

She swallowed hard. "He's only eleven. He's too young."

He shook his head. "I'm afraid not."

She sighed. "But Rick is older and bigger, and he looks mean. And you said he could even be involved in supporting his brother's drug habit. How is Justin going to stand up to a boy like that?"

"He has to learn how. Unless you're planning to hover over him all the time."

"Of course not." As much as she wanted to argue the point with David, she feared deep down he was right. She glared at the boy who looked like an overgrown bully. Still talking and scowling at each other, Justin and Rick moved toward the front of the house, out of her line of vision.

She wanted to rush out there and save the day. But maybe it wouldn't be such a good idea. Undeniably, she would embarrass Justin if she did. "Now we can't even supervise."

"Maybe Justin is telling Rick to leave."

"I hope so. Where are the girls?"

"They're fine. I left them on the beach building sand castles." He frowned. "How's your shoulder?"

She stretched and tried to roll her shoulder, but a sharp pain jabbed her.

"Let me take a look."

Turning, she lopped her yellow shirt down her back. "How does it look?"

"Painful." He began massaging her neck, his fingers warm and gentle. "Your muscles are in spasm. I'm sure that accounts for some of the pain." His strong fingers kneaded the muscles in her neck and shoulders.

Needles of pain shot from the pressure points. "Ohh. That *really* hurts."

"I don't want to hurt you, but massage will help in the long run." He slipped her swimming suit straps down over her upper arms. His hands were large and work-roughened and gentle. And his touch sent a current along her nerves that rippled in widening waves like a pebble tossed into a pool. "You did great skiing today. I told you it would all come back to you."

She beamed at the memory of her jubilation when she'd finally been able to relax for the ride. "It took long enough. But it was so much fun. I'd almost forgotten the challenge—the excitement."

"You forgot you have to build your muscles, too. You gave us a real scare."

She remembered the stricken look on her children's faces. "I could see how frightened the kids were. Sorry to put you through that." Forcing her mind off her kids and squelching her fears about Justin and Rick, she leaned into David's capable hands and willed herself to relax. His hands felt so warm. So comforting. So good. She savored the heat spreading from his fingers and sinking into her bones.

"You're right about the kids. They're so damned vulnerable. I didn't realize just how vulnerable until you fell." His fingers moved more slowly. He swept his hands gently across the tops of her shoulders and halfway down her arms, then rested his hands on her shoulders. "Nan…"

The gravity of his tone snapped her to attention. She turned to him.

He met her gaze, his dark eyes haunted. "We can't let them think—"

The door slammed.

She dragged her gaze from David's eyes.

Justin stood just inside, dirt clinging to his chest and legs, his face twisted in a watery scowl and a trickle of red seeping from his nose.

She tensed, an internal alarm jangling every nerve. Why hadn't she listened to her motherly instincts and sent that bully home? "Justin! What happened?"

David slipped her swimsuit straps into place, pulled her shirt up and withdrew his hands from her shoulders.

Missing the pressure of his hands, she struggled to shift gears into her mother mode.

"I want to go home." Justin's tight voice sounded as if tears weren't far away.

She drew her shirt around her neck and strode over to Justin. "Why were you fighting?"

He glanced at David, then glared at her. "I want us to leave."

David strode across the room. "How did Rick know you were here?"

Justin drew in a shaky breath, but he didn't answer.

She frowned at her son. "David asked you a question. Answer him."

Justin gave her a scowl as if testing the waters. When she scowled right back, he turned his scowl on David. "Rick knew 'cause my big-mouth sister had to brag about you taking us water-skiing."

"I see. Well, you'll have to deal with it, then, I guess. I'm going to have a word with Rick if I can find him." David grabbed a ring of keys from one of the hooks near the door and walked out.

Nan opened her arms to her son. He flung his arms around her and squeezed her fiercely. She savored his warmth and tried to remember the last time he'd hugged her—so long ago.

Justin sniffed. "Rick's a jerk. Can we go home?" The trickle of blood had become a stream. It covered his lip, which was beginning to puff up.

"Your nose is bleeding."

"I know." Justin bit his lip.

"Tip your head back. Let's get you cleaned up." She guided him to the kitchen and moistened a paper towel under the faucet. "Why didn't you want to talk to David? Are you embarrassed about fighting?"

"Yeah, I'm embarrassed. Can we go now?" Sarcasm tainted his voice.

"Don't you think that would be rude?" She washed away the blood on his face and chin. "Hold the towel under your nose."

Justin obeyed.

She gave him a puzzled frown. "Why were you and Rick fighting?"

Chin quivering, Justin shut his eyes. "Trust me, Mom. You don't want to know."

"You're wrong. I wouldn't ask if I didn't want to know."

He glared at her. "Rick said some stuff I didn't want to hear, so I hit him. Okay? Stuff I couldn't see because I'm such a sap."

"You're not a sap. What did Rick say?"

Justin shook his head.

Reaching for patience, she walked over to the refrigerator, took an ice cube from the freezer and wrapped it in a clean paper towel. "Have I ever done anything to make you think you can't trust me?"

"No."

"Then why won't you talk to me?" She took the soiled paper towel from him and handed him the clean one with the ice cube inside.

He screwed up his face as if considering her question. "Rick said mean stuff. Stuff Dad wouldn't want you to hear."

Her heart ached. Justin was protecting her like he believed his dad would. "Rick swore? That's what you don't want me to know about?"

"Rick's a creep. I'm not going to tell you what creeps say. Anyway, it doesn't matter 'cause Rick's not my friend."

Well, that thought brought relief.

"David isn't my friend, either, and I'm not coming out here anymore."

She drew in an alarmed breath. "Why not? Did Rick say something about David?"

Justin's chin jutted stubbornly.

She could shake him for believing anything Rick would say that could drive a wedge between him and David. "Everything has been going so well between you and David, why would you believe Rick if he did say something?"

He chewed on his lower lip, as though mulling over her question. "I'm just a charity case to him, Mom."

She couldn't believe her ears. What in the world had gotten into him? "That's an awful thing to say. David has been very good to you. To all of us."

"Maybe he's been a little too good."

"What's that supposed to mean?"

"Don't you wonder why he's so interested in us, all of a sudden?"

Where was this coming from? "He's our friend, and he's worried about you getting in trouble."

"Right. I bought that story, too. Hook, line and sinker. But not anymore." The belligerent tone was back in his voice.

Not again. Not when she'd begun to catch glimpses of her bright little boy. She had to get to the bottom of this. "Tell me what you think his motive is."

"It has nothing to do with me, that's for sure." His scowl softened. "If I promise not to get into any more trouble, can we forget we ever knew David?"

Frustration pounded vehemently behind her eyes. "Why? What do you think he did?"

"He's using us, Mom."

His words touched an angry chord within her. How could he think such a thing when all David had done was try to help? She tried hard to control her anger. Anger wouldn't help. Getting Justin to open up took patience. "What are you talking about? How do you think he's using us?"

"Can't you trust that I know some things? I'm not a little kid anymore."

She was getting absolutely nowhere. Justin no longer being friends with Rick wouldn't solve all her son's problems. He still needed help dealing with Corry's death. He needed David. And she certainly wasn't going to give up without a fight. "You agreed to work with David for a month. And you need a job so you can pay Mr. Harper for the broken window, remember?"

"It'll take me all month to make fifty bucks. Don't you have some work for me?"

She shook her head. "You gave your word, and you have to stick to your deal."

He bit his lip again, seeming to consider his options. "Well, the deal's over the end of the month. And I don't want to do any more family picnics and stuff. Working is the only way I'm going to spend time with him."

Disappointment shot through her. She'd had so much fun today. And she'd loved including the kids. David was so good with them.

Justin sniffed. "I want to go home now."

She couldn't allow him to scuttle everything. It wouldn't be fair to the girls. "We're not going home yet. I promised Brenda she could swim a little while. She watched all of us water-ski, you know. And if you won't tell me what Rick said about David, I insist you talk to David. Don't you think he has a right to know?"

Setting his chin, Justin scuffed his tennis shoe against the floor, the rubber sole emitting a high-pitched screech.

She tried again. "If you don't want to be treated like a little kid, you'll have to do things in an adult way. You have to discuss this with David."

Glowering his refusal, he turned on his heel. "I'll wait in the car."

That night Nan walked out of Justin's room after saying good-night to her silent, angry son. Every muscle she owned throbbed. She should have known better than to water-ski for more than five or ten minutes without building up her strength. The most strenuous workout her thirty-five-year-old muscles had achieved in the past two years was gardening, for heaven's sake.

But her muscles would recover. Justin's attitude was what worried her. He was a tough little boy again. Closing her eyes, she fought the dread sinking into her psyche. His suspicion of David made no sense. What could Rick have said that would make Justin angry enough to fight? And why wouldn't he tell her what it was?

When David had returned after being unable to find

Rick this afternoon, he'd accepted Justin's abandonment with the patience of Job. Such a wise, gentle, kind man. He'd make a wonderful father. Too bad he'd chosen not to be a father.

His no-nonsense approach with Justin had helped her deal more effectively with her son. But David's influence had done more than that. The confidence he'd given her had made her stronger. She thought about the strength that flowed from him so effortlessly.

The grating sound of the swing on the front porch caught her attention. She wasn't surprised. After the way they'd left David's house this afternoon, she'd figured he would stop in to check on them. Anticipation lightening her step, she strode to the front door, unlocked the screen door and walked out onto the porch. "Hi."

Still in his uniform, he met her gaze with troubled eyes. "Hi."

"I thought you might stop by." She settled in one end of the swing beside him.

"I didn't want to wake the kids with a phone call. How's your shoulder?"

She flexed it a little, a dull throb rewarding her efforts. "It's stiff. And you were right. I'm beginning to feel muscles I never knew I had. Although waterskiing was worth it."

"You'll have to exercise to work out the kinks tomorrow. And if your shoulder gives you trouble, you might have to see a therapist."

"I'm sure it will be okay."

"If it isn't, you take care of it."

"I will." She gave him a small smile, glad for his concern. He made her feel cared for.

"How's Justin?"

She dragged in a deep breath. "He's not trusting again, and he won't talk about it."

A muscle in David's jaw clenched. "Not trusting you or not trusting me?"

"Both of us, I think. Apparently, something Rick said made Justin particularly angry with you. I told him he had to talk to you about it."

"We'll get to the bottom of it."

"I hope so." She realized she was twisting her wedding ring in agitation.

He grasped her hand in his. "I'm concerned, too—about all three of the kids. The thought of something happening to you terrified them today. Hell, why wouldn't it? You're all they have."

"Yes."

"You were right. We could really hurt them if they get the idea they can depend on me always being around for them."

Nan nodded, remembering the hope in Brenda's eyes when she'd asked if he could be her daddy. And Melody might be more subtle, but she, too, hoped David would be part of their family.

"What have you told them about us?"

"That we're old friends." Old friends seemed so inadequate, but what else could she say? Technically they weren't a couple, in spite of the assumptions their friends had made. And they weren't lovers—

"Old friends? Is that what we are?"

Her heart thudded hard. "What else?"

He dropped his gaze, a small frown flitting across his face. "I wish we could be a lot more."

She found herself holding her breath as they sat in silence, her imagination running wild, the warmth of his hand seeming to scorch hers. "I wish we could, too," she finally breathed.

Blowing out a stream of air, he raised his gaze to meet hers. "I like being with you. I don't want to give that up, but—"

"Neither do I." She shut out the alarm pounding at her temples and realized she was trembling. She couldn't imagine not seeing him. She didn't want to imagine it.

He gripped her hand a little tighter, his jaw clenching. "The kids have to be our first priority."

"Yes."

He flinched, peering darkly into her eyes.

She bit her lip. "I'll explain to them why we can't be more than friends. But I don't think that will be enough. We'll have to keep them out of the equation as much as possible."

"You mean not let them see us together?"

"I know that won't work completely. But whenever they do see us together, we'll have to act more distant."

He raised her hand and held it to his jaw. "I don't know if I can do that."

She searched his eyes for reassurance, but what she saw was worry mixed with need.

"Nan, I wish circumstances were different. I wish…"

Her heart clenching in her chest, she stroked his jaw, his slight razor stubble teasing her fingertips.

He closed his eyes.

She couldn't stop herself from leaning close and pressing her lips to his.

With a low groan, he claimed her mouth as he slid his arms around her and pulled her against him.

She reached to encircle his neck, kissing him with a longing so overwhelming she was stunned.

He lifted his head and searched her eyes. "Oh, lady. What you do to me."

She gave him a smile. "I think you're the one doing the doing."

He kissed her again, gently nudging the seam of her lips with his tongue.

Melting in his arms, she opened to him. Without hesitation, he slipped inside. He tasted her deeply, stealing her breath with excitement and dizzying need. By the time he raised his head, she could barely remember her own name.

He nuzzled her neck. "You smell so good. Almost as good as you taste."

She stroked his hair, the faint scent of almond shampoo teasing her.

Raising his head, he looked down at her, his crooked grin curving his lips. "We must have been out of our minds to agree to no kissing."

"Certifiable."

But his grin faded as quickly as it had appeared. "I've wanted to kiss you for so long. I can't do the 'just friends' thing anymore, Nan."

"I know," she agreed soberly. "Neither can I."

"But I can't stay away from you, either. You're more important to me than I want you to be."

She smiled, a warm glow pushing away her worries. "You make me strong. And you give me something to smile about."

"I like your smile." He traced her eyes, her nose, her mouth with his fingertips as if memorizing her features. "So we'll see each other only after work or after your classes."

"I know it isn't a real solution, and I hate being secretive but…"

"Yeah." He studied the porch floor. "We have to do everything we can to protect the kids. But what about the Fall Festival? I told Diane I'd help you in the school fund-raising tent."

"Maybe if we drive separately? And meet in the tent."

"All right." He glanced at his watch. "It's late. I'd better leave. Shall I expect Justin to work for me Monday after school?"

"Yes."

He drew away, stood and touched her nose. "Take care of your shoulder." With that, he turned and left.

She waited until the Jeep's taillights disappeared around the corner, then she got up, walked into the house and down the hall to her lonely bed. She licked her lips, savoring the taste of David. Being in his arms was even more wonderful than she'd remembered.

Their relationship was changing in spite of their intention to keep it from doing so. And if wishes were all they needed, she wouldn't have let him leave.

Chapter Ten

David gulped down a tall glass of cold water and glanced out his kitchen window at Justin stacking chunks of wood on the woodpile. "What exactly happened, Cindy?"

The social worker sat at the table, a two-inch stack of reports in front of her. "When Justin didn't show up after school today, I called Kate McDuff, the sitter. She hadn't seen him, either. So I drove to school. He was in the principal's office sitting out detention with Rick Kellogg for fighting on the playground. Rick has a shiner and Justin has a fat lip."

At least Justin had gotten in a punch in spite of his size handicap.

"I waited for Justin and gave him a ride out here. He wouldn't say more than two words to me. I've never seen him so angry and withdrawn. That's why I had the dispatcher contact you at work. I thought maybe you could get him to talk to you."

"I'm glad you let me know. Not that I'm sure Justin will talk to me, either."

"Why not? You were making progress with him. Doesn't he approve of you and his mother?"

David jerked his head around to frown at her. "His mother?"

"I hear you took her to the Gardners' party last week."

"Word travels." The memory of Nan in his arms in her porch swing Saturday night sent heat coursing through his body. He ached to hold her, to kiss her again.

"I also heard Mike was in the bottle that night."

Pushing thoughts of Nan from his mind, he focused again on Cindy. "Mike's really hurting. You two are going to work this out, aren't you?"

She shook her head slowly, tears pooling in her eyes. "Don't start. We were talking about Justin and his mother. Do you know what happened to set Justin back like this?"

"I wish I did." He turned to the window again. Justin slammed another chunk of wood onto the pile. The kid wore only cutoffs and tennis shoes in obvious defiance of David's warning to keep covered to avoid getting slivers imbedded in his skin. Terrific.

Getting to the bottom of Justin's anger would be challenge enough, but he needed to do more than that. He needed to somehow win the boy's trust back if he was going to help him. He couldn't let Justin sink into his cynical world of distrust again. Then he'd be even harder to reach.

David might as well bite the bullet and try to get the kid to talk to him. He grabbed a couple colas from the refrigerator and strode for the door.

"Good luck," Cindy said.

"Thanks. I'm going to need it." The screen door slammed behind him, and the blistering heat of the afternoon walloped him. He gazed wistfully at the cool blue horizon. He'd give a lot right now to exchange this scratchy uniform for his swimsuit and plunge into the depths of Lake Mendota for a swim. He walked up behind Justin. "Time for a break."

Without even glancing over his shoulder, Justin jammed another chunk of wood into place.

"Come on, here's a Pepsi." He shoved the can of soda in the kid's face.

Justin accepted it glumly, snapped up the flip-top and threw his head back to gulp down half the can. He held his body stiff, his animosity emanating in waves.

David noted the puffy lip and scrape on Justin's chin. "I hear Rick has a black eye."

Justin raised his chin a little.

"Let's walk down to the lake."

Ignoring David, Justin took another long drink of soda.

David turned and strolled away, hoping the boy would follow.

He did. Head down, he soon fell into step alongside David.

"Are you going to tell me why you're so mad?" David asked.

"Why should I be mad? Just because I was dumb enough to think you wanted to be my friend?" Justin's voice seethed with sarcasm, but at least he'd decided to end his silence.

"I thought we were friends," David said quietly.

"Friends can trust each other."

"I trust *you*."

Justin glowered out at the water.

"Why can't you trust me? Because you still blame me for your dad's shooting?"

The boy stiffened even more. "Shouldn't I?"

David had a sinking feeling in the pit of his stomach. "Maybe you should."

Justin stopped and glared up at him. "How come?"

"Because I blame myself."

The boy narrowed his eyes. "Why?"

"I'll never be sure if I hesitated a second too long because I didn't want to shoot a kid." David's chest ached with the possibility.

Justin bit his lip. "Did you do the best you could?"

David blew out a breath and nodded.

"If you did your best, then that's all you could do. That's what Mom says."

David scowled. "What do *you* say?"

"You're not a liar. So I guess you did your best."

David couldn't quite believe the kid's words. "You don't blame me anymore?"

"I guess not. But that doesn't mean I'm gonna let you use me to get what you want."

David frowned. "Use you? How?"

Justin set his chin.

David stared out at the water. "Are you making a point? Or are you just throwing insults?"

"Rick saw what you're doing. You're using me to get friendly with my mother." Justin spat the words disgustedly.

Understanding took shape in David's mind. Great. He could imagine the vulgar words Rick had flung at Justin. "That's not true, Justin. I have a good time with you."

The boy scowled disbelievingly.

"Is that what you and Rick fought about today at school, too?"

"That was part of it."

"What's the other part?"

"He was telling the kids things about you and Mom. So I told him to shut up. And if he didn't, I'd tell you stuff."

"About Ben?"

Justin narrowed his eyes. "How'd you know about Ben?"

"He has a police record. Did you know that?"

Justin shook his head.

"He's into drugs. I think he's behind Rick's and Pete's robberies too. And now that Ben has a car, I'm betting he's planning to broaden his base beyond Northport. Am I right?"

Justin narrowed his eyes and met David's. "I guess

you know what you're doing...as a cop," he said grudgingly.

David suppressed a grin, knowing how much that concession cost the boy. Not exactly a vote of confidence, but a whole lot better than nothing. "My bet is that they're casing out those expensive houses closer to Madison."

The boy narrowed his eyes even more.

"Don't worry about it, Justin. They'll have a very short crime spree."

Justin seemed to mull over David's words for a moment. Then he raised his chin. "What about my mom?"

"Your mother and I were friends before your dad died. We're still friends. You should have asked me about this before believing Rick."

Justin's gaze blazed with challenge. "Why do you think I punched him? I didn't believe him. Not until I watched you rubbing Mom's back. I saw the way you looked at her. Even a dumb kid like me had to see what you're up to." He swiped at his eyes with his fist.

Oh, boy. How could David explain his way out of this? He tipped back his head and took a long, slow drink of Pepsi before he met Justin's gaze again. "I like your mom a lot, but I don't spend time with you to get closer to her. I like you. I have a great time with you, and I want to help you."

"Well, I'll work out my month and then you can forget both of us. I've already forgotten you."

Ouch. The kid knew how to fight dirty. "Looks like we're in a standoff situation."

Justin shrugged. "I guess that's how it's gotta be 'cause I don't trust you with Mom. Now, I gotta get back to work." He downed the rest of his Pepsi.

The day David let a kid dictate terms, he'd turn in his badge. It was definitely time to play hard ball. "We have some negotiating to do. I won't have you working for me if you can't trust me."

Justin scowled. He clearly hadn't expected this turn in events. "How can I pay Harper off then?"

"That's your problem, not mine. I'll have to file an amended report with the department. Obviously, I can't vouch for you if I'm not supervising you. I'll turn you over to another social worker because Cindy and I work the same cases."

A deep scowl creasing his forehead, the kid stared at him as if he couldn't believe what he was hearing.

David couldn't help feeling a twinge of guilt. But he shoved it away. This was for Justin's own good. "You can finish out your hour on the woodpile and let me know when you leave." He turned and headed for the house. He would let the boy think about his predicament.

Justin didn't move. "Can we negotiate some more?"

David stopped, reminding himself to hang tough. "How can we negotiate trust?"

"What about my mother?"

David swallowed hard. The big question. How

could he explain how he felt about Nan to her eleven-year-old son?

"Do you want to sleep with her?"

Damn. How could he answer that question truthfully? "Men and women sometimes express their feelings in a physical way. It's not a sordid thing like Rick probably thinks."

"Married people?"

"Yeah. Married people. And sometimes, unmarried people." Another painful reminder of the limited status of his relationship with Nan.

"People who love each other?"

David nodded.

"Do you love my mother?"

David drew in a deep breath. Every time he thought he'd handled a difficult question, the boy asked a harder one. "I love her as a friend, and I admire and respect her."

"Are you gonna ask her to marry you?"

David stared at Justin. Ask her to marry him? He'd never really let himself think seriously about that prospect. He wanted her, needed her in his life. But marriage? Marriage was out of the question.

"Well, are you?" Justin glared, impatient for an answer.

"Uh, I don't believe deputies should have wives and families because being a deputy is too dangerous a job."

"Because of my dad?"

He nodded. "Yeah. And because of *my* dad. He was

a police officer, too. He got killed on the job when I was four. I hardly remember him.''

Justin's mouth dropped open. ''Wow. I didn't know that. Does Mom know?''

''Yes, she knows.''

''You must think I'm really a jerk for giving her such a hard time.''

''I wasn't a model son, either. It's hard growing up without a dad. I haven't always been a deputy, you know. I got into my share of scrapes along the way.''

Justin eyed him speculatively. ''You're not just saying that, are you?''

''It's not something I brag about.''

Justin shook his head. ''You should have told me, man.''

''I didn't think it was any of your business.''

''Maybe. But I don't feel like I'm such a dumb kid if you got in trouble, too.''

David couldn't help smiling. ''You're not dumb. That's why you're working hard to stay out of trouble. So where do we stand?''

Frowning, Justin scuffed his shoe in the sand. ''I guess I'd like us to be friends. And I'd still like you to come to my soccer games. But you have to stay away from my mother.''

David doused the smile and drew in a deep breath of patience. ''Now you're using blackmail?''

The boy's eyes nailed him. ''You said you're not ever gonna get married, so what's the big deal? You stay away from my mom, David.''

Dread settled around his heart. Justin didn't know

he demanded the impossible. And as much as David needed to repair the link with Justin, he couldn't give in to his threats. He turned to face him. "You don't have the right to ask that, Justin. That's up to your mother."

David skirted the Abe Lincoln monument and strode up the sidewalk to Bascom Hall, the stalwart pillars of the majestic building somewhat reassuring in their permanence. He needed to talk to Nan.

He'd left Justin thirty minutes ago, very glad for the breakthrough he'd made with the boy. But what concerned him was Justin's ultimatum ringing in his ears. *You stay away from my mom, David.*

The knot in his stomach tightening, David shook his head. He was in the middle of a no-win situation if he ever saw one. If he continued seeing Nan in spite of Justin's disapproval, the boy would cut him out of his life. How could he help the kid then?

And as fascinating an idea as marrying Nan was, marriage had never been something he saw in his future. He'd been too focused on being a cop. And in his mind, being a cop meant not getting married. And not having a family.

He'd told Justin the decision about whether or not they went on seeing each other was Nan's. But putting her in the position of choosing between him and her son? Things couldn't get much more complicated than that.

Maybe if Justin's conviction rang false, David could handle the questions and insecurities plaguing him about his relationship with Nan. But in the back of his mind, he knew the kid was right to protect his mother.

He tried to ignore the heaviness in his chest. He and Nan needed to put their heads together and try to figure out what to do.

He took the few steps two at a time, jerked the glass-paneled door open and stepped into the imposing marble-and-oak lobby. The smell of dusty old wood hung heavy in the trapped heat. Mrs. McDuff had told him Nan's Wednesday lecture took place in Bascom Hall. All he had to do was find the right lecture hall. First floor, Mrs. McDuff had said. An amplified drone was coming from the left of the giant foyer. He strode to investigate.

The double doors stood open, probably to allow circulation of the meager supply of air in the stuffy, old building. There must be two hundred students crowding the giant lecture hall, conversing and fidgeting. A bespectacled, beleaguered professor stood at a podium, his tired voice droning over a microphone like the buzz of a bumblebee. Probably Nan would sit in the front to avoid distraction from the lecture.

He paced over to the right and up the side aisle. By the time he neared the front, the din behind him subsided and he could almost feel the curious eyes burning into his back. It was pretty hard to go unnoticed in his uniform.

He spotted her in the middle of the second row, her head bent over a notebook. The elation that poured through him at the sight of her almost swamped him. It was as if he was only half-alive when he wasn't near her. And in some very deep sense, he spent every minute waiting to be with her again.

She turned and surveyed the hall around her as if she somehow sensed he was there. He knew the second she spotted him. He offered a smile to allay her fears about Justin. Her lovely face softened in welcome and her deep-blue eyes honed in on his, sending so much excitement and joy, he could barely keep from running to her. For that moment in time, they were the only two people on earth.

"Officer, do we have an arrest going on in our midst?" asked the drone.

David flinched, apprehending two hundred pairs of inquisitive eyes straining to get a better look. The damn uniform.

Nan wouldn't be very happy with him for embarrassing her in front of all these people. "Everything is fine. I'm sorry to interrupt."

"Do you have the person you want?" The drone had taken on a booming quality that seemed to echo through the now-silent hall.

"Yes, sir."

Nan stood and sidled past the row of students toward him. Flushed, she stepped into the aisle and stretched both wrists out to him, mischief in her eyes.

He didn't get it. Then he realized she was playing to the crowd, offering her wrists to be handcuffed. He grinned. "Cute."

A few uncertain twitters, then laughter and cheers turned the hall into bedlam.

He fought the urge to fold her into his arms and kiss

her. What would she do then? Maybe he'd better not try to find out. Turning, he led the way to the back of the room and through the stately lobby. He didn't halt until he pushed the glass-paneled door open and waited for her to walk out into the late afternoon sun.

She turned to him, curiosity in her eyes. "What are you doing here?"

The knot in his gut twisted. "I had a talk with Justin."

Her curiosity turned to concern. "What did he say?"

Several students ambled by, craning their necks to size up the situation. David glanced around and spotted the bench behind the Abe Lincoln monument. He guided her to the walled, marble semicircle and sat down beside her, making sure he left a little distance between them. But her warmth, her scent invaded his senses, anyway.

"Tell me, David. You're making me nervous."

Might as well blurt it out. "Apparently, Rick made a crack about me that day at my house. Then Justin saw me massaging your shoulders and made assumptions. He thinks I'm using him to get close to you."

"Oh." She sighed, her delicate little body seeming to wilt.

He drew in an agitated breath of air. "I'm making progress with him, but he threatened to shut me out if I don't stay away from you."

She laid her small hand on his arm and peered understandingly into his eyes. "I'll set him straight about that."

He clasped her hand, her smooth skin warm as the beach on a sunny day. "He's trying to protect you. It's one of the things kids do when they lose a parent. I always protected my mother, too."

A tiny frown creased her forehead, and the caring in her eyes soothed like a balm. Her soft, wistful smile made his heart ache. "I wish I'd known your mother."

"She would have loved you. And your kids." He gazed into Nan's clear-blue eyes and wanted nothing more than to go on looking at her. Then his conscience gave him a nudge, reminding him he needed to get back on track. "Justin's right to protect you from me." He heard the resignation in his voice.

She shook her head slowly, her lovely face somber and thoughtful. "No. I don't need protection from you."

"Don't be so sure. Justin asked me about my views on marriage. He doesn't think my intentions are honorable."

She drew in a deep breath and looked away. "Honorable or not, I want to see you."

Her quiet assertion zinged straight to his heart. He wanted to kiss her with the joy of knowing she wanted to be with him, too. But instead, he clenched his jaw until it ached.

She met his eyes. "We can't let Justin blackmail us, for heaven's sake."

"It's not only Justin. The last thing I want to do is hurt you and your family. But everything is so damned complicated." He realized he was stroking her hand and tried to stop.

She clasped his hand. "We need to protect the kids. And we agreed we'd keep them out of our relationship. I've already had a serious talk with the girls about us. And I'll make sure Justin understands. He will have to accept it, that's all."

She seemed convinced it would all work out. But would it? "I know we can't let him get away with dictating terms to us, but he still worries me."

She squeezed his hand. "I'll explain that neither of us wants marriage."

He blew out a breath.

"Are you on duty?"

"Not anymore. I got Paul Gardner to cover my shift for me."

Her eyes crinkled in a smile. "It's such a lovely evening. I might be convinced to skip class and go for a swim with you. It would be fun, and it would give my shoulder some exercise."

He grinned. Swimming always helped him straighten out his mind. And swimming with Nan would be a dream come true.

Chapter Eleven

Uneasily, Nan eyed her reflection in the rustic mirror in David's bathroom and shook her head. She'd called Kate to let her know where she'd be. To avoid the hassle stopping at home to pick up her swimming suit would have created, David had offered her a suit Cindy left at his house.

But the skimpy suit would never do. She hadn't worn a bikini for years, and she felt far too self-conscious to wear one now.

But what else could she do? She certainly couldn't let a swimsuit keep her from swimming with David. She slipped on her red T-shirt and pulled it down to midthigh. Much better.

David had gone upstairs to change into his swimsuit and would probably be waiting for her by now. She opened the door and strode to the deck to join him.

He stood gazing out at the horizon, graying with dusk, his strong masculine hands grasping the deck rail. In blue swim trunks, his bronze physique radiated power from his broad shoulders and well-muscled back and arms to his sinewed legs. A man of action.

She stepped close and ran her hands over his back.

Smiling, he turned and took her in his arms. "Did the suit fit?"

"Barely." She grinned, melting against him. "Literally. It's that kind of suit."

"You sure don't need covering."

"You might be disappointed." Her voice had dropped a couple of octaves since she'd last used it.

"Not much chance of that."

She looked into the depths of his dark-chocolate eyes. The promises there drew her into a world where all things were possible. A world where she could fully partake of his promises without holding back. Without concern for the future.

She leaned closer to brush her lips to his. His arms tightened around her as he claimed her mouth. Catching her breath, she entwined her arms around his neck and kissed him back. Heat enveloped her in a rush of longing.

When he lifted his head, he trailed sweet, tantalizingly slow kisses from her ear, along her neck, until he honed in on the pulse point at the base of her throat. She dragged in a shaky breath and stroked his smooth, broad shoulders.

He lifted his head and gave her a little smile. "You

kiss like an angel.'' The huskiness in his tone under-
scored the intensity in his gaze.

She lifted a teasing brow. ''You've kissed angels?''

He grinned. ''Not until I kissed you.''

She laughed. ''Ready to go for a swim?''

''Yup.'' Holding hands, they ran down the steps and
jogged to the lake's edge.

She dipped her foot in to test the temperature of the
water. ''It's cold.''

''The air has cooled, but the water won't be bad
once we're in.''

Taking his word for it, she waded in, the waves
sending goose bumps slithering over her body.

''Are you planning to swim in that T-shirt?'' He
gave her a questioning frown.

''It will keep me warmer.''

''You're kidding, right?''

She heard the disbelief in his voice. He'd think she
was a total prude. Well, she *was* kind of a prude.

He grinned his lopsided grin. ''Serious swimming
will be cumbersome in that shirt. No need to be self-
conscious. Nobody will see you but me.''

Therein lay the problem. If she saw disappointment
in his eyes, she'd die. But if she was too uptight to
take off the darn shirt, what would he think? She
grasped the bottom of her shirt, hiked it over her head
and tossed it to the beach.

When she turned to him, he stood perfectly still
while he allowed his eyes to roam from top to bottom
and back again. She swallowed, afraid to try to read

his expression. "There's a reason I don't wear bikinis, you know. Having babies kind of changes things. And I must admit, I really haven't exercised like I should. Somehow, I never seem to find the time. But I hope to do better, if I can just—"

"Shh." He touched his finger to her lips. Cupping her chin, he tilted her head so she had to look into his deep, smoldering eyes.

She saw approval there. That and desire.

"You are the most beautiful woman I've ever seen."

Her knees wavered as if they might give way altogether.

He bent his head and gave her a quick kiss on the lips, then he grasped her hand and led her deeper into the cold water.

When it was deep enough, she lay back and floated away. Kicking vigorously, she stared up at the sliver of moon rising in the darkening sky.

"Do you think your shoulder will tolerate a race to the big rock?" His voice held the light edge of challenge.

She remembered the rock he meant and flipped onto her stomach. "You're on, but give me a head start."

"Okay, get moving."

Gliding forward into the crawl, she sliced through the water, adrenaline giving her an extra push.

David thought she was beautiful. And the desire in his eyes made her believe it. And she wanted to satisfy his desire. She wanted the passion she tasted in their kisses. And not only the passion. On some level, she wanted to give him whatever he needed...and receive all he had to give.

Twinkling lights beckoned on the other side of the lake as David raced Nan to the rock about two hundred yards out. They rested, and she challenged him to race back to shore. Watching her stroke, her body gliding through the water, made him happier than anything he remembered. Thoughts of sliding his hands over her slippery wet skin sent him to the moon.

He envisioned her standing uncertainly in the bikini. She had no idea how beautiful she was. He'd been unable to tear his eyes from the swell of her breasts and the way her waist nipped in above her flat stomach. He'd had all he could do to keep from molding his hands around her fullness and bending to taste her breasts.

Even now, the relentless tension burned in his muscles. But swimming with her was fun and a sure way to keep his hands off her.

Extending his arm in a powerful stroke, he turned his head to grasp a breath of air and to glance at Nan. Where was she? She'd been right beside him seconds ago. Halting midstroke, he spun to look for her.

In the dim glow offered by the moon sliver and the sky full of stars, he spotted her just behind him, floating on her back. "Your shoulder giving you trouble?"

"A little."

He turned onto his back and floated beside her.

"Look at all those stars."

He gazed up at the star-studded sky. A beautiful

night, all the more so because he could share it with her. He couldn't remember ever being so happy. "Seems like we're suspended in time out here, doesn't it?"

"It's wonderful. I'd almost forgotten how much I love swimming. And it's such good exercise. I need to do it more often."

He smiled with the fantasy of her swimming beside him every day.

When they got back to the beach, he stood up in waist-deep water and waded alongside Nan, floating on her back, kicking languidly. She sat up in water past her ribs, its buoyancy mounding her breasts high and full.

He closed his eyes and waited for a wave of longing to ebb.

She tried to stand, but she kind of folded back into the water.

He offered his hand to pull her up.

"My legs are rubbery." She grasped his hand. Her skin was cold, and she shook like a leaf in a squall. "I definitely need more exercise."

Without further thought, he swooped her into his arms. Her little body felt so light, her wet skin slippery against his. He held her as tightly as he dared and strode for shore.

She laughed her soft laugh, her warm breath fanning his cheek. She squirmed in his arms. "I'm too heavy."

Reveling in the feel of her body against his chest, he tightened his grip. "You're light as a feather. But quit wiggling, or you'll slide out of my arms."

Settling her hand on his shoulder, she smiled into his eyes. "If you're trying to impress me with your strength, it's working."

Even though her skin was cold, her touch burned into his shoulder like a branding iron.

She looked up at the sky, her neck an open invitation. "I think there are even more stars out now. It's such a lovely night. So peaceful and quiet."

The soft caress of her body as he walked, the swell of her breast against his chest excited and tantalized him. Tension flowed into his muscles until he trembled with the force of it. He walked onto dry sand, dreading the thought of setting her down. He leaned forward to allow her to get her footing. He straightened.

But he couldn't get his arms to release her.

She turned her head and looked into his eyes, holding his gaze as firmly as he held her. She stroked his jaw, her touch barely a whisper.

He inclined his head and hungrily sought her lips.

Her breath warm and sweet, she turned to him. Her breasts pushed against his chest, the pressure of her lips permitting, no, inviting him to intensify the kiss.

And the world rocked off its axis.

He covered her mouth with his, urgently pushing at the seam of her lips, and she opened to him. She tasted like honey and sunshine. He feasted. Hungrily, greedily. He couldn't get enough. He wanted more.

And she gave him more.

He buried his fingers in her silky curls while he spun dizzily into space with nothing to anchor him to reality except her.

Soft, generous, passionate. She was all those things. And there was no hesitation in her kiss, nor in the way she melded her body to his. She gave herself freely.

And he accepted. He couldn't help himself. He needed all she would give. And she gave him the power to give in return.

Because she needed, too. He knew by the surrender in the way she clung, by the appeal in the way she stroked, by the way she yielded to him, then matched the thrusts of his tongue. And he desperately wanted to fulfill her needs. Fleeting thoughts drifted in a sea of nuances of pleasure fed by her touch, her taste, her body. He allowed his hands to explore her smooth back, her round hips.

He wanted to take her to his bed, to wake up beside her in the morning. Trying to shove the thought of her in his bed away, he ended the kiss and gazed into her eyes. "You're wonderful." He hardly recognized the growl as his own voice.

"You, too," she answered breathlessly. She caressed his face, trailing her fingers over his forehead, down his jaw. She touched his chin. "I love this little cleft."

"Yeah?" A glow of pride suffused him as if he'd been personally responsible for putting it there.

She smelled like flowers and cold lake water and Nan. Her scent, her taste, her soft body infused him with energy. Delighted him in so many ways.

She pulled back and ran her hands over his chest, tangling her fingers in his chest hair, the sensation sending sparks of electricity darting every which way, awakening his hunger for more. She bent her head and kissed his chest, her lips fluttering over him like a butterfly.

Shutting his eyes, he pulled in air and reveled in her attention. He'd thought his heart couldn't pound any faster or harder. He'd been wrong.

He clenched his hands into fists to keep from reaching for her. He didn't want her to stop. He wanted her to be free with him. He loved her wanting to please him.

When she began lavishing kisses down his stomach, he drew in a sharp breath, his muscles clenching beneath her lips. He reached for her and pulled her close.

She laid her hand along his jaw, her rapid warm breath caressing his face.

He needed more. So much more. He sought her lips, struggling to slow himself down, to take time to discover her. But the moment their lips touched, he began free-falling. Clasping her face in both hands, he claimed her lips with the pent-up frustration he'd struggled to contain. Blood rushed in his ears as his ability to reason faded. He drank of her sweetness like a man dying of thirst.

They took turns exploring the depths of each other's mouths and roamed each other's bodies with urgent hands. Dragging in air, he sank to his knees in the sand, pulling her down with him. He pressed her to him, the sensation knocking the breath out of him.

She gave a soft little sound.

The pressure of her delicate body fed the raging fire

in his blood. Finally he broke the kiss. "I can't seem to let you go."

"I don't want to go anywhere." Her voice was low and soft and filled with so many promises.

Promises he could no more refuse than he could disavow his pounding desire. Lowering his head, he nestled hot kisses across the swells of her breasts above the bikini top.

"Your kisses are dynamite," she said breathlessly. She ran her hands through his hair and arched her body to give him freer access.

Did she have any idea how hard he had to struggle to keep from throwing good sense and conscience to the winds and laying her down right here in the sand? "I want you...so much," he breathed against her silken breast.

Before he realized what she was doing, she peeled the top of her suit off and her lovely, full breasts rose and fell in the moonlight.

Raising his eyes to hers, he saw uncertainty there. His heart swelled to overflowing. She was offering herself to him, and she wasn't sure what his reaction would be. He smiled. "You're more beautiful than I could have ever imagined."

She returned his smile a little shyly.

Holding her gaze, he molded his unsteady hands around her fullness and grazed the hard nubs with his thumbs.

She took a quick little breath and arched toward him.

He bent his head and took her nipple into his mouth.

Hot urgency slammed through him, driving him fast and hard.

She gripped his shoulders while he worshiped her breasts with his mouth and hands, her muted sounds enticing him to higher and higher levels of ecstasy. Amazing, the excruciating pleasure that welled up in him when she sighed or gave a little gasp or moan. Never before had a woman's pleasure driven him to such heights. Somewhere in the heavy haze of unquenchable desire, he realized she was trembling. He lifted his head. "You're shivering."

"It's you. Your hands...your mouth... There ought to be a law against what you do to me."

The ache to please her almost overwhelming, he claimed her breasts with fervor. She gave a little cry, then buried her fingers in his hair and clasped him closer. He almost went wild, suckling and nipping with abandon while she gave and gave some more. Each little moan, each little movement drove him closer and closer to abandoning all thought of control. She was magnificent. He wanted to take her—yes. To possess her. To own her. He'd never wanted like this.

He laid her in the sand. Running his hands down her smooth curves from her underarms to her hips, he fitted her body to his. Perfect.

She shifted to cradle his desire more intimately.

He groaned, his body thrusting without his permission. He reached for her swimsuit. Hesitated.

Then reality hit him.

What in the hell was he doing? He had no protection. He couldn't make love to her without protecting her. And that wasn't all. Even if he had protection, he couldn't make love to her on the beach like a randy teenager. He'd never forgive himself. She deserved so much more.

"What's wrong?" she whispered.

Hauling in a tortured breath, he rolled into the sand beside her, his entire body screaming in protest.

"David, please." Turning to him, she laid her hand on his chest, her touch burning into him. "I want you to make love to me."

"I don't have protection." He grasped her hand and clasped it to his lips.

"Oh." Fluttering kisses over his chest, she reached lower to stroke him gently. "Do you have anything in the house?"

He groaned, unable to breathe with the exquisite sensations reverberating through him. He tried to think about her question. "Yes, I think so."

"Shall we go inside?" Kissing his stomach now, she grasped him and stroked.

He sucked in a breath, his body surging to savor her attentions. "Good idea," he moaned, reaching for her. Struggling to his knees, he scooped her into his arms.

Draping her arms around his neck, she nestled her head on his shoulder and kissed his neck. "I think we'd better hurry," she whispered.

Chuckling, he lifted her into his arms as he climbed to his feet. And hurry he did. Across the beach, into the house, up the stairs. Which was anything but easy with her soft breasts burning his chest, her hands fondling his head, her lips kissing his neck. Finally he lowered her onto his bed.

"I'm all sandy," she said breathlessly.

"I don't care, do you?" He ground out the words and set to work peeling her out of the bottom half of her suit.

In answer, she reached to tug down his swimsuit.

"I'd better do that." He'd shatter if she touched him right now. He slid the suit down and kicked it off.

"Oh, David," she whispered, her eyes wide as she stared at him in the soft moonlight filtering through the curtainless windows. The awe in her voice gave him an unneeded shot of adrenaline.

He collapsed beside her, snuggling his face to suckle her breast as he smoothed his hand over her stomach and lower to stroke her with his fingers.

Shuddering, she arched her back and clasped his head tightly to her breast, her soft moans more and more urgent, her body more and more restless. "I need you…"

He stretched to reach the bedside table and snared a condom. His hands shook as he quickly sheathed himself. When he'd finished, she opened her arms to him, her eyes luminous. With a strangled groan, he lowered himself over her, burying his length in her welcoming warmth.

"Perfect." She smiled up at him, running her hands over his chest.

"*You* are perfect." His voice was as ragged as his nerves.

"I can feel your heart pounding," she murmured, her voice hushed and intimate.

"I think it's about to break a rib."

Stretching and raising her arms to encircle his neck, she pulled him to her.

He kissed her as he began to move in an age-old rhythm.

She raised her hips and wrapped her legs around him.

He thrust hard and deep, her tight little body driving him wild. He kissed her neck, her eyes, her nose and settled on her lips. She nipped his lip and soothed the sting with her tongue.

Fighting for control, he captured her mouth, thrusting his tongue inside in rhythm with his thrusts into her body.

Her breath coming in sharp, little pants, she rocked with him, meeting his thrusts. The powerful tide of release threatened to overcome him. He fought it off.

"David—" The shimmering plea in her voice went straight to his core, driving passion he could no longer contain. With a fierce growl, he drove deeper, desperate to fill her. Desperate to get his fill.

A low scream rose from her throat. He shattered in a blinding storm of sensations as he captured her sounds in his mouth, unwilling to share her, even with the night.

Chapter Twelve

Nan stood in the middle of her living room, savoring the lingering taste of David and the dull ache of satiated desire deep within her body.

She'd immersed herself in him. Kissed and touched his smooth bronze skin until she couldn't breathe with longing. She'd lain in his strong arms, taken him into her emptiness, and he'd fulfilled her deepest needs.

But she still wanted him desperately. Trembling with the exhaustion of consummation, she touched her fingers to her swollen lips. He'd done more than awaken her dormant libido. He'd set her on fire.

Leaving him had been wrenching. Neither of them had known what to say, and the heaviness of knowing they could never return to mere friendship lay between them like a weight. Where had her common sense been when she'd needed it? After being in his arms tonight, how could she go back to her lonely half existence? She couldn't. She shook her head.

But how could they go forward? What in the world were they going to do? She absentmindedly switched off the light and walked down the dimly lit hall, stopping to check on the girls.

Melody lay sprawled on her stomach, her tousled blond curls springing disobediently around her peaceful face. One arm entrapped her aging ''Tuddy,'' the giant stuffed bear Corry had shown up with the first day of Melody's life.

Nan's heart flooded with love for her firstborn child, almost a woman physically but still clinging to her childhood teddy bear for bedtime security. She bent and kissed Melody gently on the cheek.

''Night, Mom,'' Melody murmured without stirring.

''Night, hon.'' She turned to Brenda's bed, seeking her dark, little head snuggled among the countless stuffed animals. Bending, she pulled the blanket up over Brenda's small shoulders, kissed her lightly on the cheek and walked out of the room.

Brenda no longer abandoned her own bed to climb into Nan's the moment Nan nodded off. She missed Brenda's warm, Mr.-Bubble-scented body cuddling close, but she was relieved her little girl could finally sleep without fear.

Nan walked into Justin's room, stroked Sheba's purring head and bent to kiss Justin on the cheek.

"You're very late." He lay flat on his back, staring up at her.

She jumped, startled. "Why aren't you asleep?"

"I was worried about you."

She drew in a deep breath. She needed to talk to him, but preferably not tonight. It was too late, and she was too off balance. "I'm fine. Get some sleep, okay?" She turned and strode to the door.

"Were you with David?"

She paused. She couldn't lie to Justin. "Yes."

"Don't see him anymore."

Without turning, she drew in a shaky breath. She'd have to talk to him now. He wasn't giving her a choice. "That's for David and me to decide. It doesn't involve you. Is that clear?"

"But Mom...he told me he doesn't think cops should get married."

She turned to face him. "I know that, Justin. I don't plan on marrying him, either. Do you think I'd do that after Daddy was shot because he was a deputy?"

Justin sniffed.

She had to be firm and she had to make this crystal clear. "I have fun with David. I like being with him. But that's all I want. You don't need to worry about me, okay?"

No reply.

"There's no reason for you to be angry with him. Do you understand?"

"Maybe," he said grudgingly.

"He cares about you. I want you to be nice to him. Is that clear?"

"Yes," he answered grudgingly.

"Good." She turned and trudged down the hall and into her empty bedroom.

She closed the door, slumped down on the bed and switched on the lamp on the bedside table. She loved her kids more than life. Since Corry's death, they'd almost filled the void. Then why this excruciating loneliness now? Her children were safe, secure and here with her.

She dragged in a shaky breath.

David.

Her arms, her heart, her soul yearned for him. She thought about the warmth and caring in his eyes. About the smile that lit his face when he looked at her. Scrolling through her emotions, she tried to sort them out. What *did* she feel for him? Admiration, respect, trust. Desire, of course. And awe that he wanted her, too.

She remembered the urgency in his warm hands, the passion in his kisses, his trembling restraint. She moaned with the intensity of longing raging through her.

She pressed her cool hands to her hot cheeks, then gazed down at her wedding ring. *Corry, you know I'll always love you, but I'm so lonely.*

So lonely that she'd made love to another man. But loneliness hadn't pushed her into David's arms tonight. She'd wanted him. And she had wanted him for some time. She sighed, waiting for guilt to pounce. But it didn't materialize.

Corry had loved her. He'd want her to move on with

her life. And David had given her the strength to move beyond fear to embrace life again.

That's why she'd given herself to him so completely tonight. That's why she couldn't imagine her life without him.

She slipped the plain gold band off her finger and kissed it. Placing the ring in the carved jewelry box on the dresser, she stared at it through her tears.

Tears of loss. And of discovery. Of pain. And joy. And life.

Rolling his shoulders to ease the ache between his shoulder blades, David drove the squad car down the highway toward the county garage. In the dim light of the dashboard, he glanced over at Mike deep in thought in the passenger seat. Mike looked tired, and he'd hardly said two words all night.

Not that David had minded. He'd been more than content to linger in his haze of excitement after making love with Nan last night. Making love with her had done nothing to curb his craving. It had increased his hunger a thousandfold. He was impatient to hear her voice. All he could think about was how she'd sounded when they'd made love. About how much he wanted to hear her, taste her, feel her again.

He signaled a left turn, his mind's eye filled with Nan dozing in his arms after their lovemaking. So beautiful. So passionate. She'd been more than he'd ever imagined a woman could be. She'd given so willingly, so completely. She'd driven him far beyond anything he'd ever experienced, and given him total completion as though making love with her united his body and soul.

When she'd stirred and smiled up at him, he'd wanted to make love to her again, but she'd had to hurry home to her kids and her waiting sitter. After she'd left, he'd lain in his bed alone, her scent taunting him.

"You and Nan Kramer hitting it off?"

He jumped. He'd forgotten Mike was in the car. Worse, he realized he had a wide grin plastered on his face. But the last thing he planned to do was to discuss Nan with Mike. "We're doing okay." The understatement of the decade. "You still living in Waunakee?"

"Yeah. But I hope not for long."

David glanced over at Mike. "You and Cindy are patching things up?"

"We're trying. She called last night to tell me she was giving notice at work today. That she was going to move back to Los Angeles to be near her family. I couldn't let her go."

David grinned. "So?"

"I raced over there and told her, and we talked the night away. We agreed to see a counselor. Turns out neither one of us is ready to give up on our marriage. And hell, if having a kid makes her happy, maybe I could live with it."

David pulled the car into a parking stall and killed the engine. "Then you're quitting field work?"

"No. I'm not a desk jockey, Dave. Any more than you are."

He shot Mike a frown. "But if you have a baby—"

"I'm still not a desk jockey. Cindy knows that."

"I can't see why you'd risk not being around for your wife and kid."

"I guess I'm not the fatalist you are. I'm a cop. You, of all people, understand what that means."

David swallowed into a dry throat. Yeah, he understood all right. Hadn't he used that argument with Justin? "I'm glad for you, Mike."

"Thanks. We're not home free, but I must admit life is looking a whole lot better." Mike shoved open the squad car door, climbed out and slammed the door behind him.

David followed suit and strode for his Jeep, uneasiness creeping up his backbone. So maybe Mike and Cindy could come up with a compromise that would work for their marriage. Why should that bother him? Because it was a compromise he'd never make?

But that hadn't stopped him from making love to Nan, had it? He'd scrapped their friendship and compromised her peace of mind, knowing he had nothing to offer her for the long term. Knowing he was jeopardizing the tie he'd established with her son.

Uneasiness had settled in the pit of his stomach by the time he strode into his house and slammed the door against the wind howling off the lake. He shrugged out of his uniform shirt and hung it over the back of a kitchen chair, then stepped out of his trousers, creased them carefully and hung them over the back of another chair. Grabbing the portable phone, he took the steps two at a time on his way to fetch some clothes.

He needed to talk to Nan. He needed to see her. He needed to touch her. Maybe the uneasiness would let up then.

Shaking his head, he glowered at the phone in his hand and set it on the bedside table. It was after midnight, for crying out loud. He couldn't call her. Anyway, he wasn't ready to talk to her. He still hadn't figured out what to say.

Without thinking, he pulled on his swim trunks, then raced down the stairs and slammed out the door. Once outside, he headed for the water. What he needed was to swim until exhaustion drove away his pounding need for Nan. Maybe then he could think.

But before he reached the beach, he heard the thunder of waves crashing the shore. He stopped at the water's edge and stared at the breakers battering the shoreline. What was wrong with him? A strong north wind had moved in during the day bringing an autumn nip with it. The temperature didn't bother him, but the wind churning the water made swimming impossible.

He stood, glowering at the foaming waves.

All he could think about was being with Nan. Touching her. Kissing her. Making love to her again. Waking up beside her in the morning. Every morning.

Every morning?

Imagine never having to leave her. Being there for her whenever she needed him.

He shook his head. He was the worst possible man for her. A deputy, for crying out loud. The worst possible man to help her raise her kids. As much as he'd like to believe his concern about the dangers of his job were unfounded, deep down, he knew no one could predict what might happen out there. Look at what had happened to his dad, to Corry.

But Mike was right about desk duty. David never had been able to stomach it.

He turned and strode back to the house. He stalked up the stairs like a raging bull. Flopping on his back on the bed, he grabbed a pillow and drew in a deep breath of her scent. He groaned with the need suffusing him. He replaced the pillow and stared at the ceiling, trying to focus his mind on figuring out what to say to her. On what to do next.

The ring of the phone startled him. He picked up on the second ring.

"David?" Her soft voice spoke hesitantly in his ear.

His heart lurched and careened out of control. He sat up. "Hi."

"How are you?"

"Fine. You?"

"Good. I'm good." She sounded as if she was trying to convince herself.

His heart contracted until he couldn't breathe. "Are you sure?"

"I'm fine. I know it's awfully late, but will you come over?"

"I'll be right there."

"See you soon." She hung up.

His heart thudding in his chest like a beached trout, he set the phone on the table. Heaving himself off the bed, he tugged off his swim trunks, pulled on jeans and a gray sweatshirt as he stepped into loafers. Then he strode down the steps and out the door.

The closer he got to Nan's, the faster his heart danced. He was powerless to slow it down. Pulling up to the curb, he glanced at her darkened house, only a dim light glowing through the screen door. He strode to the porch, climbed the steps and spotted her sitting in the big wooden porch swing. As he walked across the porch, she stood. He folded her in his arms, crushing her to him as if he hadn't seen her for days.

Clasping her arms around his neck, she laid her head against his chest.

He stroked her silky hair. They stood holding each other in the darkness. He kissed the top of her head. "I love holding you."

"Mmm. You do it so well," she said, nestling closer.

He grinned, a surge of pride nudging his ego. He held her for a long time while wholeness seeped into his being. "Was Kate okay with last night?" he murmured into her hair.

"She assured me she was. She's a romantic at heart." Her soft voice was muffled against his chest.

He pulled back a little and looked down at her. "What about you? Are you okay with last night?"

She tipped back her head and gazed up at him, her eyes shining. "Last night was wonderful."

He swallowed around a lump in his throat. "It's not what we planned."

"No, we didn't. But it *was* wonderful." She gave

him a questioning look as though wondering if he was having second thoughts.

"Wonderful is too bland. How about stupendous? Fantastic? Amazing?"

She laughed low and deep.

He loved her laugh. Bending close, he kissed her softly on the lips. He drew in her taste, ran his hands over her back and settled them possessively on the soft curves of her hips because he could. But it wasn't enough.

Pulling her close, he deepened the kiss.

With a low moan, she tightened her arms around his neck and melded her body to his.

He crushed her to him, thrusting his tongue into her mouth, and she answered his thrusts. He wanted her. Here. Now.

But he reached for reason. Reason and self-control. Slowly and by sheer force of will he ended the kiss. "Stupendous, fantastic, amazing," he quipped, his voice as raspy as an old saw.

"And more," she said breathlessly.

"I've needed to kiss you all day." He kissed her neck, drew in her scent. "And kissing you isn't all I've been thinking about. We need a little more privacy than your front porch allows, though. Even in the wee hours of the morning."

He sat down in the swing and pulled her onto his lap, the pressure of her little body edging him toward overdrive. "We could go to my place, but I doubt Kate would appreciate a call at this hour, even if she is a romantic."

She wrapped her arms around his neck and gazed into his eyes. "Justin was awake when I got home last night."

He drew in a guilty breath. "Oh, boy."

"I set him straight about his trying to dictate whether or not we see each other."

"But his problem isn't with you. It's with me."

She combed her fingers through his hair. "I made sure he knows I'm not planning to marry you, either. That I could never marry a deputy after what happened to his dad, but that I enjoy being with you. I think he understood."

He ran his hand over her back. "The problem is, I *can't* stay away from you."

She stroked his face, her touch soothing and smooth. Smiling, she trailed her fingers over his nose, then caressed his lips.

He caught her fingers in his mouth and sucked on them.

She laughed softly and ruffled his hair with her free hand.

His heart pounding with delight, he caught her hand and wound his fingers through hers. She had wonderful hands. So small and delicate and silky. And bare.

He glanced at their interlocking fingers. At her ring finger in particular. "You took off your wedding ring."

She looked at him very seriously. "Yes."

For an instant his heart forgot to beat. Quiet exultation coursed through his blood. He hugged her close. Burrowing his head on her shoulder, he kissed her neck. She smelled like heaven. His senses drank her in. Her warmth, her delicate softness.

But guilt and disquiet prodded his mind and grew until it challenged his joy. The significance of her removing her wedding ring both elated and terrified him. Why was he surprised she'd no longer consider herself married after last night? But did taking off Corry's ring mean she'd changed her expectations where David was concerned?

No. She'd told Justin she'd never marry another deputy. So why was he worried? She knew he couldn't meet her need for a safe, secure life. Neither her need nor her children's.

But he couldn't stay away from her. Just being near her fed him in ways he couldn't name.

"A penny for your thoughts, David."

He raised his head and gazed into her shining blue eyes. She was here, in his arms. Nothing else mattered. "You know my thoughts, beautiful lady." Shoving aside his doubts, he sought her mouth.

Chapter Thirteen

Bright lights flashed and noise from the rides on the midway assaulted Nan's ears. The scent of grilled hamburgers and cotton candy mixed with the chilly fall air inside the pie and ice cream tent. She handed a paper plate filled with pie à la mode to a chubby man who looked as if he ate a lot of desserts. "Enjoy," she said, taking his money and turning to put it in the cash box on the table behind her.

She walked over to David as he intently scooped ice cream onto a slice of pie. He wore jeans and a black turtleneck that outlined the powerful muscles in his shoulders and arms. He grinned at her, and her legs turned to jelly. Then he strode away to give the pie to a customer.

She loved his being here with her. Just as she'd been

delighted when he'd shown up at Justin's soccer game this morning. Of course, she'd tempered her delight for her daughters' eyes. And Justin certainly hadn't invited David to his soccer match for her benefit. She pushed away the cloud of uneasiness threatening to spoil her euphoria.

She was so restless to feel David's arms around her. Working beside him was fun, but it was also a challenge to remember not to touch him. Not to run her hands down his back. Not in public, for all Northport to see.

If she didn't want to be the topic of discussion at church tomorrow morning, she needed to keep the nature of her relationship with David under wraps. And she especially needed to guard against her children thinking he would be a permanent part of their lives. She couldn't hurt them that way.

David returned, wiping his hands on a paper towel. "How long are we scheduled to work?"

"Diane said she'd be here a half hour ago. Sorry you signed on for this gig?"

He grinned and met her eyes. Bending closer, he spoke quietly. "It's fun, but I'd rather be on your front porch with you. Or better yet, at my place."

Yes, yes, she wanted to shout. But instead, she gave him a smile and nodded her agreement. She glanced at her watch. "I need to round up the kids and get them home to bed as soon as Diane and Patrick relieve us."

"Before you round up the kids, I want to—"

"Hey, you two, how about a couple pieces of that apple pie with ice cream?"

She turned at the sound of Paul Gardner's voice. He and Susan stood smiling like two clams. Nan shot David a look and grasped two plates of apple pie, holding them out for him to embellish with ice cream. Pie in hand, she donned a perky smile and strode to the beaming Gardners.

"How's business?" Paul asked.

She set the pie down in front of them. "We've been very busy all evening."

"Nice of you to help Nan out, David." Susan looked past Nan.

"Happy to. It's for a great cause," David answered.

"And what are good friends for?" Susan fixed Nan with an amused smile.

She forced herself to return the smile. No point in getting in a huff about Susan's teasing, especially when Susan was right about David and her. Not that she planned to confirm Susan's suspicions. Their relationship was nobody else's business.

Diane swept into the tent and donned an apron over her pregnant belly. "Thanks, guys. I planned to be here sooner, but our two-year-old took forever to settle down tonight. Looks as if you sold lots of pie."

"Where's Patrick?" Nan didn't want to leave Diane unless she had help.

"He's finding a parking place, but he'll be here shortly, and we'll finish out the night. Scoot."

"Thanks. This is a wonderful fund-raiser." Nan

took off her apron and laid it on the back table, then followed David out of the tent.

"Have fun, you two," Susan called, an annoying lilt in her voice.

Nan ignored her and made sure to allow distance between David and her as they walked away. "Susan's in her glory."

"What do you think she'd do if I kissed you right here and now?" David grinned his lopsided grin.

"Don't you dare."

"Maybe we should give her and the good people of Northport something to talk about."

She shook her head and laughed. "Our working together in the tent will keep them occupied enough."

"When do I get to kiss you, then? If we can't let the good folks of Northport see us, and we can't let the kids see us…" He raised a teasing brow.

"What about all those kisses on my porch the past two nights? Aren't you getting your fill?"

"Not even close. Are you?" He gazed into her eyes, his longing mirroring her own.

She shook her head, the memory of their heated kisses and stroking hands giving her a flutter. And she wanted more than kisses. But her front porch called for a certain amount of decorum even late at night. That and the fact that her children could wander out of bed at any moment had kept David and her in control.

"Let me take you for a ride on the Ferris wheel? Nobody can see us kiss on the top. And with any luck, we'll get stranded up there."

"It sounds like a wonderful idea, but it's getting late. I need to find the kids."

"I'll help you find them. Right after our Ferris wheel ride."

She laughed. "You won't accept no for an answer, will you?"

He shook his head. "Indulge me?"

Her heart melted. He *had* spent four hours dishing up pie and ice cream for the school fund-raiser, for heaven's sake. "Okay. One Ferris wheel ride before we head home."

His grin spreading, he clasped her elbow and guided her down the noisy, bustling midway toward the giant wheel.

She loved feeling his touch on her arm. But it wasn't enough. Not nearly enough. Nothing was ever enough with David.

"Hi, Mom and David." Melody waved from a booth where a group of girls clustered. A sign over the booth read "Win a giant panda. Three balls for a dollar."

David took his hand from Nan's elbow and stepped away from her.

"Mommy." Brenda ran to them, water sloshing over the sides of a small, glass bowl. "Melody won me a fish."

Nan bent to admire the tiny goldfish. "It's very nice."

"I named him Kermit. See, David?"

He peered into the bowl. "Nice to meet you, Kermit."

Brenda giggled.

Nan's heart swelled at his easy camaraderie with her daughter. He'd make such a good father. A pang of regret pierced her heart. "We're heading home in about twenty minutes, girls. Meet me by the pie and ice cream tent. And tell Justin, if you see him," she called, as she and David walked away.

She couldn't help a twinge of guilt. It was past her kids' bedtimes. But at least they could sleep a little later on Sunday morning.

David bought two tickets for the Ferris wheel, and they were lucky enough to get into a short line. He stood behind her, resting his hands discreetly on her hips, his warm breath ruffling her hair. Her nerves humming as they always did when he was near, she turned and smiled up at him.

Giving her a grin, he splayed his hands over her hips and pulled her against his hard body.

A tremor of desire shuddered through her. His heat seeped into her, and she struggled to keep from laying her head back against his chest. Instead, she glanced around to make sure one of her kids wasn't watching. Or Susan Gardner.

Soon they reached the head of the line. The controller steadied the seat for them. They climbed aboard, David stretching his arm along the seat behind her. Up they swept, the noise and people fading far below. High above the crowd, the air held even more of a chill. She shivered, her expectant heartbeat accelerating as they approached the top.

Right before they reached the zenith, he leaned over

and captured her lips for a very brief, very intense kiss that took her breath away. As they swept over the top and began to descend, her entire body leaped to life. He lifted his head, and all she could do was smile into his dark eyes, her heart fluttering like a wild thing. "Are you sure people can't see us?"

"Not at the top. All they can see is the platform our feet rest on. Trust me. I've researched this."

She laughed as they went flying down into the noise and confusion. They dipped near the ground and started climbing again. It was almost as if they were on a floating, fantasy island, beyond the cares and concerns of everyday life.

Nearing the top, she stroked his thigh, and he bent close, his lips claiming hers, his hand caressing her breast. Over the summit they swept and began their descent.

David lifted his head, his eyes dark with desire. "Oh, lady."

Her heart beating frantically, she gave him a smile. "You take my breath away."

"I'd like to take the credit, but I think it's the Ferris wheel."

"You're too modest. My heart is beating way too fast."

"The height." He grinned and cocked a brow. "You think so?"

"Must be. I'm having the same problem. Probably everyone on the wheel is suffering similar symptoms."

She laughed. "I doubt that. Maybe we should experiment to determine what exactly is causing the problem.''

''A great idea.'' They approached the summit, and he dipped his head close.

Chuckling, she stopped him. ''No kissing this time. This trip will be our control factor.''

He groaned. ''I'm afraid I don't have much control where you're concerned. But anything for science.''

They crested the top.

''I'm experiencing a slight breathlessness, but no heart flutters.'' She grinned.

He laid his hand on her breast over her heart. ''Funny, I feel fluttering.''

She drew in a quick breath. ''No fair.''

Chuckling, he clasped her hand and placed it over his heart. ''You be the judge. Any flutters?''

His heart pounded sure and steady and strong under her fingers. ''No flutters, but lots of pounding.''

They swept low and began to climb again.

''The pounding is my control slipping.'' He drew her hand to his lips.

''Oh-oh.''

Up they swept. Just before the summit, he drew her into a clinch and kissed her so hard she couldn't breathe. Liquid heat suffused her, making her limbs languid, her mind foggy. They were well over the top before he let her go. When he did, she couldn't separate from him. She was so wrapped in desire, she could only lean into him, wanting, needing.

Around the wheel swept, beginning its climb again.

Hazily she looked out at the crowd and tried to regain her sense of reality.

In one terrible instant, her gaze locked with her son's.

He stood a short distance away, a look of betrayal and utter disbelief clouding his countenance. His face crumpling, he turned and ran.

"Justin. No, Justin," she yelled, half standing, the seat rocking forward precariously. She had to stop him. She had to explain. She felt David's arms around her, pulling her back as the wheel swept up, leaving her little boy far below.

"Where is he?"

She pointed. Tears clouded her vision of Justin running blindly through the crowd, bumping into people, pushing ahead as fast as his eleven-year-old legs would carry him.

The Jeep's tires squealed as David took a wide curve in the road. *Be there, Justin.* If the kid hadn't gone to his place, he didn't know where to look next. They'd scoured the carnival grounds, and the boy hadn't been home when David had followed Nan and the girls. Nan had tried to play down her worry for the girls' sakes, but he saw the fear in her eyes.

He didn't blame her. He was damned scared himself. It was close to midnight and Justin was just a boy, a very upset boy who might do something stupid and get himself into serious trouble.

David drew in a deep breath. This was all his fault. Where had his mind been when he'd coerced Nan into going on the Ferris wheel? He knew damn well where his mind had been. Working beside her all evening had built such a fire in him, he couldn't stand the idea of letting her go home without his kissing her. He should have had more sense, but any sense he'd ever had disappeared when she was near.

A feeling deep in his gut told him Justin would need to vent. He sure hoped so. He pulled into his driveway, jumped out of the Jeep and strode around the side of his house.

Justin's bike lay sprawled in the sand beside the deck. Relief almost swamping David, he climbed the steps and spotted Justin slumped on the edge of the chaise lounge. "Hey, Justin."

The kid sat glaring straight ahead.

Raking his hand through his hair, David tried to figure out where to begin to build a bridge to the boy. He shoved his hands in his pockets. "Did you ride your bike out here in the dark?" A rhetorical question, but a reasonably safe one.

Justin gave a quick nod.

Not a great decision on Justin's part, but they'd talk about that later. "You must have wanted to see me pretty bad."

The boy drew in a shaky breath and seemed to fold into himself even more.

"I guess you're really angry with me." David sat down beside him, his heart aching.

Tears rolled down Justin's cheeks. He ignored them.

"Since you're here, you might as well tell me what you came to say."

"You don't know what you're doing, man." Justin's words were low and seething with contempt. "You're gonna really hurt my mom."

David closed his eyes against the pain stabbing him. Leave it to Justin to cut to the heart of the matter. If only he could deny the boy's accusation. But deep in his heart, he couldn't deny the kid wielded the dagger of truth. Wearily shaking his head, he blew out a stream of air and opened his eyes. "I wouldn't hurt your mom for the world."

Turning toward him, Justin glowered his rage. "I saw how she looked at you."

"Oh, Justin." He wanted to reassure the kid so badly, but he didn't know what to say. He certainly wouldn't instill confidence if he told him he'd lost all control of the situation.

"You're doing what Rick said. You're using her and then you're gonna leave." A little sob punctuated his words.

David shifted his gaze to the deck floor. "I would never use her, Justin. I care too much about her."

"You sure aren't worrying about her."

Justin was wrong there. He'd worried himself sick, but all his worry hadn't done one bit of good. His need for Nan had still taken precedence over everything else.

"Have you thought about what will happen when you leave her? Where will she be then?"

"I don't want to leave her." His voice sounded strangled. The thought of leaving her choked the life out of him.

"Have you changed your mind? Are you gonna marry her?" A tinge of hope replaced the sting in Justin's voice.

David swallowed hard and squinted at the boy, his heart so heavy he couldn't breathe.

"You're gonna leave her, aren't you?" Justin exploded. "Don't lie to me." He glared at David, daring him to deny his words.

But he couldn't deny Justin's words.

If he still believed deputies had no business marrying anyone, let alone being a dad, didn't that mean he'd eventually leave? What other choice was there?

He stared into Justin's angry and frightened eyes, and the truth hit him full force.

He'd run out of time. The only thing he could do was what he should have done a long time ago. He had to walk away.

Nan's heart heavy with guilt and regret and a deep sense of dread, she settled in the porch swing beside David. He'd brought a silent, tear-stained Justin home, and her son had gone straight to his room. How had she let things get so totally out of hand? She had acted irresponsibly, and her son was paying the price.

David stared straight ahead, tension emanating from him. "I'm sorry, Nan. I should have used better sense."

She drew in a quick breath that sounded like a whimper. She laid her hand on his arm. "*We* should have used better sense."

He turned to her. "We can't ignore the problems between us anymore."

"No." Pretending their problems didn't exist had exploded in their faces. She reached up and ran her fingers gently over his eyelids, his nose, his mouth. She wanted to soothe away his tension, to go on touching him forever.

"Don't. Please." His voice was a deep growl.

Closing her eyes against the pain stabbing her heart, she folded her hands in her lap.

"I never should have gotten close to you." His voice was flat.

She tensed, chills chasing through her body. "I don't feel that way."

"You need a safe man. Not a deputy. Not me."

She shook her head. "I don't want a safe man. I want you."

"How would you live with the uncertainty of never knowing I'm safe after what happened to Corry?"

"I don't know. All I know is I can't go back to the emptiness that was my life before you. You give me strength. You chase away my loneliness and coax me to leave sadness behind."

"What about the kids?"

She didn't have an answer.

"Your kids need security. They need to feel safe. I can't give them that. And they deserve a mother who isn't torn up with worry about whether I'll come home in one piece. You deserve a man who can give you what you need to make you whole."

"*You* make me whole."

He shook his head, the pain in his dark eyes burning into her soul. "Your family does that. And I can't be part of your family."

She grasped his arm. She needed him. As part of her family. As part of her life. As part of her soul.

She loved everything about him: his strength and energy; his gentle humor; his concern for her children; his empathy for her confused, angry son; his sensitivity for her budding teenage daughter; and his gentle patience with Brenda.

She loved him. And not only as a friend. She'd fallen in love with him.

She allowed the knowledge to sink in, and she embraced the wonder of it. Love was a miracle.

But how would she ever live with the uncertainty of never knowing if he was safe?

How had she lived with that fear with Corry?

Suddenly she knew the answer. She'd lived with the fear by letting it go and concentrating on the love.

And she could do it again.

"I love you, David."

He closed his eyes as if to shut out her words. "Please, don't say that."

"It's true whether I say it or not."

A muscle clenched in his jaw.

Tears stung, her heart swelling with love for this brave, gentle man. "No matter how much I want to keep my world well ordered and safe for my children, I love you. I can't change that. I don't want to."

"I can't be what you need."

"You *are* what I need. What we all need."

He shook his head.

"No matter how much pain Corry's death brought, I'd never give up a minute of our time together. What's important is to live fully every day we have, and I can't live fully without you."

He stood up, paced to the porch steps and stared out at the street. "You'd live every day in fear. After what you and the kids have been through, I can't inflict that on you. I won't." He sounded so definite. So final.

Tears blurring her vision, she stood and walked to stand beside him. "You think you're protecting us. But can't you see? Being with you is worth any risk."

"I would only hurt you more as time went on. I'm sorry, Nan."

"You can't give up on us. I won't let you."

He winced. "This is the first right decision I've made where you're concerned." He drew in a labored breath, but his words held the power of conviction without compromise. He jogged down the steps and strode toward his Jeep.

Pain twisted inside her, and sobs surged for release. Tears blinding her, she turned and stumbled into the house. When she reached her bedroom, she shut the door and let the tears flow.

Drawing her hand over her face, she caught the almond scent of David's hair. Her David. Warm, loving, gentle man who drove her to ecstasy and filled her soul with love.

She'd given him her heart. And without him, emptiness was all she had left.

Chapter Fourteen

Adrenaline pumping, Justin watched the soccer player from the opposing team give the ball a hard kick. Justin crouched as the ball sailed straight for his goal. He stopped it with his head, then scurried after it and gave it a mighty kick down the playing field. But before he could regain his position, an opposing player sent the ball hurling back, low to the ground like a deadly missile heading straight for the goal.

His heart in his throat, Justin threw his body. He felt the thud of contact, but had it been solid enough to stop the ball? He heard the crowd cheering. But for which team?

"Nice going, Kramer."

Recognizing Coach's voice, Justin grinned. He'd made the save.

"Way to go, Justin," his mom yelled above Melody's and Bethany's squeals.

Pretty proud of himself, he climbed to his feet, automatically surveying the sidelines for David. He'd be blown away by the play Justin had just pulled off.

Then he remembered. David wasn't here.

Which didn't seem right. Not when David had taught him that play. And David had been the one who'd pushed him to go out for soccer in the first place. Heck, without his coaching, Justin would never have made goalie.

It just wasn't the same without David cheering him on. Nothing was the same without David.

Justin had been wrong about him. He was a good cop and a good guy all around. He'd done the best he could to save Dad. Yet he'd been honest enough to admit he made mistakes, even when Justin hadn't made it easy. If it wasn't for David, Justin might have let Rick bully him into working for his brother. Without David, he wasn't sure he would have been brave enough to stand up to Rick.

And Justin wasn't the only one who missed David. His sisters did. And last night, he'd caught Mom crying. She was so sad all the time, even when she pretended she wasn't.

David had plowed into their lives whether Justin wanted him there or not. He'd made Mom and everybody need him, and then he'd left them all hanging.

He set his chin. Maybe it was time to let David know exactly what he thought.

* * *

David shivered against the wind blowing off the lake and took a few pieces of mail from his mailbox. Glancing down the road, he saw a lone biker headed his way. As the biker drew a little closer, he recognized Justin.

Heart aching, he let out a deep sigh. He didn't want to see Justin or anybody else who reminded him of the Kramer family. Of Nan. He hadn't even trusted himself to drive by her house since the night he'd left her standing on the porch.

Shoving the mail into the back pocket of his jeans, he walked around the side of the house and headed toward the lake and the roar of the waves crashing the shoreline.

Justin soon joined him sans bike.

"Your soccer game over already?" David asked.

"Yup. We won. Man, you shoulda seen the save I made. Just like we practiced."

Pain wrenched David's heart. "I'm sorry I missed it."

"Yeah. Me, too." Justin kicked at the sand.

David clenched his jaw and tried not to remember the hurt and betrayal in the boy's eyes that night on his deck. It would haunt him the rest of his life. Just as the sadness and hurt in Nan's beautiful eyes haunted him.

He realized his hands were balled into fists. He wanted to slam something. He shut his eyes and willed his pounding heart to slow down.

"Man, you don't look so good. You're as sad as

Mom. I know she thinks about you. A lot.'' He gave the sand another kick and bit his lip. ''I've been thinking…I was probably wrong telling you to stay away from her.''

David drew in a deep breath and let it out. He should have had as much sense as this kid. ''You were right, Justin.''

''Because you're a cop?''

''Yeah.''

''Why do you have to be a cop?'' The kid's chin jutted, his eyes challenging.

''We've already had this conversation. A cop is who I am. I don't know any other way to explain it to you.''

''But what if Mom loves you?'' Justin glowered at him as if he expected a profound answer.

David shut his eyes again. He didn't have any answers. All he had were questions.

''Hey, you love Mom, too, don't you?''

He didn't have the energy to deny it. He closed his eyes, hoping the kid would give it up.

''That's it, isn't it?''

The kid was treading way too close to the truth. ''You don't know a damn thing, Justin.''

Justin narrowed his eyes. ''Liar. I saw my mom crying last night. If you love her, how can you make her so sad?''

David felt sick inside. ''Don't do this.''

''My dad left because he didn't have a choice. But you do.'' Justin squared his slight body as if ready to fight.

Pain stabbed David's heart. ''Leave it alone.''

"You don't know what love is."

Justin never knew when to quit. Anger seethed deep inside David. "What makes you such an expert on love? Experience?" Cringing at his own bitter tone, he shut his eyes. Now he was using sarcasm on the poor kid.

"I know if you really loved my mother, you'd do anything to make her happy." Justin stomped off toward his bike, his back stiff with indignation, his self-righteous judgment fouling the charged air.

What did an eleven-year-old know about adult love? Everything seemed simple to Justin because he saw things in black-and-white. No shades of gray. No conflicting emotions or motives or goals. He probably believed in happy endings.

David knew better. He'd never known a happy ending.

He watched Justin ride off, then trudged into the house and threw a couple more chunks of wood on the fire. Shivering, he felt as bleak as the landscape and almost as cold. He'd never been more miserable. And the weather wouldn't even allow him to swim to relieve the stress.

Slumping onto the couch, he felt a jab. He reached into his back pocket, withdrew the mail and tossed it on the couch beside him. A creamy envelope caught his interest. Nan's distinctive handwriting grabbed his attention.

Adrenaline slammed through his body like a lightning bolt. Damn, he missed her. Would the pain never go away? Heart pounding, he grasped the envelope and ripped it open with unsteady hands.

A whelk seashell in soft watercolors decorated the front, but Nan's fluid writing drew his eye to the bottom of the card. Her letters were generous and graceful just as she was. "You never hear the miracle…" He opened the card. "…Until you listen with your heart."

His heart clenched and tears stung his eyes. Drawing in a shaky breath, he read on. "Happy Birthday. We hope you are well. We miss you. Love—Nan, Melody, Justin, Brenda and Sheba, too."

Tomorrow *was* his birthday. He'd forgotten, but she hadn't. Longing overpowered him. She'd given him the happiest days of his life.

His life held little meaning without her. His heart just couldn't seem to recover. Would he ever be happy, or whole, or give a damn about anything again?

He'd been treading water since the night he'd walked away from her, struggling to just stay afloat. Any fool knew a swimmer couldn't survive treading water. It devoured every calorie of energy until the exhausted swimmer sank. Hell, he had barely enough energy to get through a day.

And the nights. He couldn't sleep. When he did doze off, nightmares tortured him. They always involved Nan and her kids in some grave danger. He merely watched from a distance and did nothing.

What held him back? Commitment? No, he'd never had trouble committing. It was the fear of hurting those he loved, that's what it was. He wanted to protect them. And Justin was right. He loved Nan. And he loved her kids.

Nan had told him she loved him. If she was as miserable as he was, just how was he protecting her? He shook his head. He wasn't.

He was protecting himself.

Because he also loved being a cop. He loved the excitement of the chase, the satisfaction of a good collar, the pride of knowing he was making a contribution to the world.

He'd told Justin a cop was who he was, but he hadn't become a cop until after his mother died. He thought about his mother's pain after his father was killed. About her loneliness and disappointment after her marriage to Joe, a dull man who went to bed every night at eight-thirty. Joe was safe, but he hadn't made his mother happy. And he hadn't been the father David needed, either.

Could David make Nan happy? Could he be the father her kids needed?

Even if he could be what she needed—what the kids needed—what gave him the right to Corry's family? Just because he'd lived instead of Corry?

Nan had once told him to focus on why he'd lived instead of why Corry had died. Was she right? Could David have lived to love and take care of Nan and the kids?

The heaviness in his chest eased. "Oh, God. How I want to believe that."

But how was he going to take care of them? He'd never be happy as a desk jockey. And he couldn't work in the field. He wouldn't do that to Nan and the kids.

Justin's words tormented him. *If you really loved my mother, you'd do anything to make her happy.*

Anything.

There had to be a way. All he had to do was figure out what it was.

Sheba's tail at full mast, the cat mounded her back and meowed. Nan glanced at the door. A tall, dark shadow loomed outside the curtained window. A light rap sounded on the door. No doorbell. Thank heavens. She hoped the kids had finally fallen asleep.

Who would visit at ten o'clock at night? She smiled. Not all that long ago, a late-night visitor would have sent her into a tailspin. She strode to the door. "Who is it?"

"David."

Her heart stopped beating. She couldn't breathe. She fumbled with the dead bolt, her shaking fingers finally grasping and turning. She pulled open the door.

He towered on her porch in jeans and an ebony Fisherman sweater, the soft glow of the porch light highlighting his dark hair. A frown hovered over his rich brown eyes. He opened his mouth as if to say something, but no words materialized. He licked his lips and drew in a long breath.

She waited, emotions crowding for recognition. Joy. Laughter. Sadness. Anger. But longing and love overwhelmed her and drove tears to the surface. She willed them away.

"Can I come in?" His deep, gruff voice sent shimmers skittering along her nerves.

She stepped aside. "Of course. You're always welcome at the Kramer house." She hoped her voice conveyed lightness. Her heart pounded so loudly in her ears, she couldn't be sure. What was he doing here?

He eyed her uncertainly. "I practiced a speech, but I can't remember the words."

Her breath caught in her throat. "Just give me the highlights."

"Well…it began with 'I love you.'"

She drew in a quick breath, tears springing to her eyes. Her silly heart stopped beating again. Trembling began deep inside and spread through her.

"And it ended with 'I love you.'"

She hurled herself at him and threw her arms around his neck.

He inhaled sharply and folded her into his arms. "I've worked out a plan."

Of course he had a plan. He never would have come without one. Her David protected those he loved, no matter what. And he'd found a way for them to be together.

"I figured out how I can be a cop without being a desk jockey. I'm scheduled for the exam to make sergeant. I want to train new recruits. And I'm not going back in the field."

She frowned. "But you love being a field deputy."

"I love *you* more." He claimed her lips in a kiss to build a dream on.

Stroking his hair, she reveled in his scent, his

mouth, his strong arms, his hard body. She soared with joy. David was home.

He crushed her to him, deepening his kiss.

She yielded to his tongue while he drove all thoughts from her mind. Breathing became a challenge. Her knees turned to jelly. She hoped he'd catch her when her legs gave out entirely. He ran his hands down her back and pulled her closer.

She heard her own soft moan. She should probably stop this. She didn't know how.

Finally he ended the kiss and held her tightly.

She couldn't catch her breath.

"Wow. The explosive potential of my obsession." His low, breathless murmur reverberated against her ear.

"What did you say?"

"A lifetime ago, I decided I needed to face you and defuse the explosive potential of my obsession."

"Why would you want to do that?" Her words rode a puff of air.

"Crazy idea. I gave it up."

"Thank heavens." She nuzzled kisses along his neck, drawing in the fresh scent of his aftershave.

"I'll never get through my speech if you keep doing that."

"Is your speech more important?"

He silently kissed the top of her head.

She leaned back to look up into his dark, serious eyes.

"I'm sorry I hurt you, beautiful lady."

"I can't deny it. I've been miserable since the night you walked out of my life."

"I thought you needed a safe man."

She frowned in distaste. "I told you I didn't want a safe man. I want *you.*"

So much love shone in his eyes, her heart ached. Still holding her close with one arm, he held a small, gold foil package tied with a blue ribbon in front of her. "I bought you something. Open it."

She accepted the sturdily wrapped little package. "Did you wrap it?"

"Can't you tell?" He gave her his lopsided grin, his eyes crinkling.

She swallowed around a lump in her throat. Nothing lit up her world like his smile. "It's beautiful. I like that you wrapped it for me."

"Yeah?" He touched his fingers to her cheek.

Tearing her eyes away, she focused on the tiny package.

What would he buy her? She could hardly wait to find out. She slipped the ribbon off and carefully lifted the taped ends of the paper to find a pretty blue box inside.

He took the paper and ribbon from her.

She lifted the hinged cover. Nestled in lapis velvet lay an exquisite gold ring shaped like a whelk seashell, its long conic tail wrapping to form the ring, its spire sparkling with a swirl of tiny diamonds. She caught her breath. "It's beautiful."

"I know it's unusual for an engagement ring, but—"

"Engagement ring?" She stared at him, wide-eyed. Obviously, she'd missed something.

He blew out a breath of air. "I'm getting this all botched up." Holding her gaze, he released her and dropped to one knee. "Nan Kramer, will you marry me?"

Her heart stopped beating again. Those darn tears blurred her vision, and she so wanted to see David. "Yes, I most certainly will marry you."

A grin spread over his face.

She leaned to kiss him full on the lips.

She felt his strong arms drawing her onto his thigh. Slipping her arms around his neck, she kissed him with all the yearning she'd held back for so long. Her only thoughts were of him and a safe place to lie with him. But first she had to breathe. She ended the kiss and dragged in air as if she'd run a three-minute mile.

He honed in on her neck, his hot kisses feeding her hunger. "You drive me crazy," he murmured against her neck. "If I can stop kissing you long enough, I want to put my ring on your finger."

"I'd like that." This whole thing seemed like a dream, and she couldn't bear to think she might wake up. She unwound herself from David and straightened as properly as she could and still maintain her balance on his thigh. She gazed at the delicately crafted ring. "It's exquisite."

"The wedding ring kind of folds into the design. There's an inscription inside." He took the ring from the box and handed it to her.

She read. "You have my heart." The words blurred. Those darn tears again.

"It's my answer to your birthday card. Remember? 'You never hear the miracle until you listen with your heart.'" He touched her cheekbone to stop a tear. "I want the miracle."

Drawing in a shaky breath, she handed the ring to him.

He took her left hand in his and kissed her ring finger. Then he unsteadily slipped the ring onto her finger.

"Perfect," she whispered, her heart full enough to burst.

He drew her close and held her. "Do you think Corry would understand?"

She stroked his hair. No one but David would ask that question. She swiped at the tears flowing freely now. "He loved us. I *know* he'd understand."

"How long do you think it will take the kids to get used to the idea of us getting married?"

"About a minute."

"What about Justin?"

"Less than a minute."

"Then let's get married next week."

She pulled back to look at him.

He frowned. "I don't want to wait any longer. I need you beside me when I wake up every morning."

"Next week will be perfect. But I want to marry you no matter what you plan to do, you know."

"With you to come home to, I'd be nuts to take

any more risks than I have to. I plan to be around for a very long time.''

"But will you be happy not being a field deputy?''

"Very happy. I'll have more time to learn to be a dad. I figure the challenge of a field deputy's job is a piece of cake compared to being a dad the Kramers can be proud of.''

She studied him.

"And I'll have more time to work with teenagers. Counseling teens gives me a lot of satisfaction. I've even thought about starting a business in the future to do that. 'Saveteens.' How does that sound?''

"'Saveteens.' I like that.''

"Maybe you could get your degree in counseling, and we could be partners in business, too.''

"Have you worked out a plan for our whole lives?''

"I thought I'd wait for your input for that. But I do have a few ideas.''

"For instance?''

He smoothed his finger over her bottom lip, his gaze locking intently with hers. "I love your kids, you know that.'' He paused as if trying to find the precise words. "When the time is right, how would you feel about having an Elliott baby?''

David's baby. And she'd thought her heart couldn't get any fuller. She lay her hand along his strong jaw, smiling through her tears.

"Yeah?''

She nodded. "I'm not dreaming, am I? Because if I am, I never want to wake up.''

"Would telling the kids make everything real?''

She beamed and hugged him. He understood her needs better than she did, this gentle brave Adonis of hers. Finally she stood up.

Arms around each other, they walked down the dimly lit hall to wake the kids.

Epilogue

"Keep the noise level down, kids. Remember, this is a hospital. Mothers and babies are sleeping," David admonished. An excited Melody, Justin and Brenda in tow, he strode down the long corridor with more than a little pride in his step. He couldn't wait for the kids to get a glimpse of their new baby brother who had made his entrance into the world just before midnight last night—exactly a year since David had proposed.

"Here we are." He nudged open the door and peeked inside. She sat in bed, gazing down at their son in her arms. He grinned, his eyes misting as he thought about coaching her through the baby's birth last night. He wouldn't have believed he could love her any more than he already did. But last night had proven him wrong.

The silent kids stood close to him, seemingly intimidated by the importance of the moment.

Nan looked up, a radiant smile spreading over her lovely face. "Hi, gang. Come over here and meet your new brother."

All three kids surged past him, noisily arriving at her bedside.

"He's so little," Melody exclaimed, leaning to peer at the baby's dark, fuzzy head. "I remember when Brenda was born. But she was never this little."

Nan laughed her soft laugh. "She was even smaller, Melody. But you weren't very big then, either."

"David said he's a boy baby, and I wanted a girl like me and Melody." Brenda puckered her forehead in an accusing frown.

"But you and Melody have each other, honey. Don't you think it's fair for Justin to have somebody?" Nan reached to stroke the little girl's rosy cheek.

Brenda cocked her head to one side and considered her mother's words. "I guess so," she conceded, touching the baby's tiny hand with a cautious finger.

Nan looked at Justin, who still stood at the foot of the bed. "Come see your brother."

Drawing in a nonchalant breath for effect, Justin sauntered a few steps closer, squinting as he ran his gaze over the small bundle. "What's his name gonna be?"

Nan looked up at David and smiled. "We've decided to name him after David's father. Mitchell David."

Justin nodded. "It's a good name, as long as we can call him Mitch."

Nan raised her brows and questioned David with her eyes.

He grinned. "Why not? Mitch sounds like a man's man."

Opening his eyes, the baby seemed to focus on Justin as he waved his tiny fist in the air.

Everybody laughed.

"Hey, Mitch. You know me already, don't you?" The confidence and pride in Justin's voice tugged at David's heart.

The kid had come a long way. He'd forged a strong bond with David, as strong as any father and son—a hard-won bond David prized and guarded, just as he prized his relationships with the girls.

But he'd be the first to admit this past year had been a challenge. He'd made sergeant, had adapted to training recruits without a hitch, and his counseling docket was jammed with teenage boys. But learning to be a father the Kramers could be proud of had been the biggest challenge. And he had yet to learn Nan's infinite patience in dealing with three energetic kids.

No doubt about it, he'd had some adapting to do as the chaos of family life took over his single lifestyle. He'd realized right away the insanity of not installing walls in his house. Before he'd been able to move Nan and the kids into his Lincoln Log house, as Brenda referred to it, he'd had to add some walls and build a second sleeping loft so the kids each had a bedroom.

Probably the most valuable thing he'd learned over

the year was not to sweat the small stuff—like the timing for an Elliott baby, for example. It was considerably sooner than he'd planned, but he wouldn't change it for the world.

Nan unwrapped the swaddled infant, and four heads bent to examine his tiny feet and toes.

Watching and listening to his little family's excited chatter, David's heart swelled with love and pride. How he'd ever been lucky enough to marry Nan still amazed him. She was the most incredible woman on the face of the earth. Each new day, she brought him new joy, and the nights were never long enough.

As if sensing his outpouring of love, she raised her head and met his gaze.

Never before had he seen heaven in a woman's eyes.

* * * * *

From

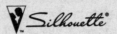

SPECIAL EDITION™

The next romance from Marie Ferrarella's miniseries

Born to heal, destined to fall in love!

Available December 2004.

THE M.D.'S SURPRISE FAMILY

SE #1653

by Marie Ferrarella

Raven Songbird came to neurosurgeon Peter Sullivan for a consultation—and before she knew it, Raven fell in love with the reclusive doctor. Would this free spirit convince him that they were destined for happiness?

Available at your favorite retail outlet.

Visit Silhouette Books at www.eHarlequin.com   SSETMDSF

This December,

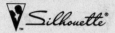

SPECIAL EDITION™

presents the emotional conclusion to

DARK SECRETS. OLD LIES. NEW LOVES.

THE HOMECOMING

by reader favorite

Gina Wilkins

Beautiful, sheltered Jessica Parks was determined to
rescue her mother from the mental asylum she'd been
imprisoned in years ago, but her controlling father was
equally intent on stopping her. Private investigator
Sam Fields had been hired to watch Jessica's every
move, and before long, she didn't mind having
those sexy green eyes zeroing in on her.
Could she turn his private investigation
into a personal affair?

Available at your favorite retail outlet.

Visit Silhouette Books at www.eHarlequin.com

SSETH

Coming in December 2004 from

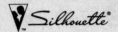

SPECIAL EDITION™

and award-winning author

Laurie Paige

The latest book in her exciting miniseries.

SEVEN DEVILS

Seven cousins—bound by blood, honor and tradition—bring a whole new meaning to "family reunion!"

A KISS IN THE MOONLIGHT

(SE #1654)

Lyric Gibson had fallen hard for handsome Trevor Dalton a year ago, but a misunderstanding drove them apart. Now she and her aunt have been invited to visit the Dalton ranch in Idaho, and Lyric is elated. The attraction between them is as strong as ever, even with their rocky history. Lyric is determined to win back Trevor's trust—and his heart—at any cost!

Don't miss this emotional story—only from Silhouette Books!

Available at your favorite retail outlet.

Visit Silhouette Books at www.eHarlequin.com

SSEAKITM

Coming December 2004 from

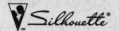

SPECIAL EDITION™

and reader favorite

Sharon De Vita

RIGHTFULLY HIS

SE#1656

Max McCallister had given Sophie the greatest gift—
the children her husband, his brother, hadn't been able
to give her. But not long after Max became sperm donor
and Sophie gave birth, his brother died. After years of
hiding his feelings for the woman he'd always secretly
loved, had the time finally come for Max to claim
what was rightfully his—Sophie and
his twin daughters?

Available at your favorite retail outlet.

eHARLEQUIN.com

The Ultimate Destination for Women's Fiction

For **FREE online reading,** visit
www.eHarlequin.com now and enjoy:

Online Reads
Read **Daily** and **Weekly** chapters from
our Internet-exclusive stories by your
favorite authors.

Interactive Novels
Cast your vote to help decide how these
stories unfold...then stay tuned!

Quick Reads
For shorter romantic reads, try our
collection of Poems, Toasts, & More!

Online Read Library
Miss one of our online reads?
Come here to catch up!

Reading Groups
Discuss, share and rave with other
community members!

For great reading online,
visit www.eHarlequin.com today!

INTONL04R

If you enjoyed what you just read,
then we've got an offer you can't resist!

Take 2 bestselling
love stories FREE!

Plus get a FREE surprise gift!

Clip this page and mail it to Silhouette Reader Service™

IN U.S.A.
3010 Walden Ave.
P.O. Box 1867
Buffalo, N.Y. 14240-1867

IN CANADA
P.O. Box 609
Fort Erie, Ontario
L2A 5X3

YES! Please send me 2 free Silhouette Special Edition® novels and my free surprise gift. After receiving them, if I don't wish to receive anymore, I can return the shipping statement marked cancel. If I don't cancel, I will receive 6 brand-new novels every month, before they're available in stores! In the U.S.A., bill me at the bargain price of $4.24 plus 25¢ shipping and handling per book and applicable sales tax, if any*. In Canada, bill me at the bargain price of $4.99 plus 25¢ shipping and handling per book and applicable taxes**. That's the complete price and a savings of at least 10% off the cover prices—what a great deal! I understand that accepting the 2 free books and gift places me under no obligation ever to buy any books. I can always return a shipment and cancel at any time. Even if I never buy another book from Silhouette, the 2 free books and gift are mine to keep forever.

235 SDN DZ9D
335 SDN DZ9E

Name	(PLEASE PRINT)	
Address	Apt.#	
City	State/Prov.	Zip/Postal Code

Not valid to current Silhouette Special Edition® subscribers.

Want to try two free books from another series?
Call 1-800-873-8635 or visit www.morefreebooks.com.

* Terms and prices subject to change without notice. Sales tax applicable in N.Y.
** Canadian residents will be charged applicable provincial taxes and GST.
   All orders subject to approval. Offer limited to one per household.
   ® are registered trademarks owned and used by the trademark owner and or its licensee.

SPED04R   ©2004 Harlequin Enterprises Limited

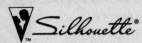

COMING NEXT MONTH

#1651 THE TRUTH ABOUT THE TYCOON—
Allison Leigh
When tycoon Dane Rutherford sought out his own form of justice,
getting involved with a beautiful woman was the last thing on his
mind. Yet Hadley Golightly was unlike other women—she taught
Dane to value the greatest gifts of life. But could her love now keep
him from the revenge he sought?

#1652 THE HOMECOMING—Gina Wilkins
The Parks Empire
Jessica Parks was determined to rescue her mother from the
mental asylum she'd been unfairly committed to years before.
Jessica's father had secretly hired P.I. Sam Fields to watch his
daughter's every move, but pretty soon she didn't mind having those
sexy green eyes zeroing in on her. Could she turn his
private investigation into a personal affair?

#1653 THE M.D.'S SURPRISE FAMILY—Marie Ferrarella
The Bachelors of Blair Memorial
The tragic death of loved ones left neurosurgeon
Peter Sullivan resistant to any kind of personal happiness.
But then Raven Songbird came to Peter for her brother's medical
care, and he found himself wanting more out of life. Was Raven
his second chance—or did she have demons of her own?

#1654 A KISS IN THE MOONLIGHT—Laurie Paige
Seven Devils
Lyric Gibson knew she loved blue-eyed rancher Trevor Dalton,
but a bumpy past kept them apart. And when Lyric found three
orphans in need, she required Trevor's help—and a marriage of
convenience—to save them. She was determined to win back his
trust.... Could his heart be far behind?

#1655 WHICH CHILD IS MINE?—Karen Rose Smith
Their babies had been mixed up at birth, and now Chase Remmington
had come to claim the daughter he'd never known. Chase knew he'd
have to share the little girl he'd lovingly raised—but could he open
his heart to the child's newfound mother, too...?

#1656 RIGHTFULLY HIS—Sharon De Vita
When Max McCallister agreed to donate sperm to his infertile
brother and his sister-in-law, he relinquished all parental control—
even though he had always had a thing for the mother of his
children. But when his brother died, Max knew it was time to
claim what was rightfully his—Sophie and his twin daughters....

SSECNM1104